Praise for *Ollie Oxley and the Ghost: The Search for Lost Gold*

"This hilarious and heartwarming adventure will have readers on the edge of their seats rooting for Ollie and thrilled by an ending that is as satisfying as the treats for sale at Cook's Candy."

—Wendy McLeod MacKnight, author of *The Frame-Up* and *It's a Mystery, Pig Face!*

"[A]n engaging story full of mystery and mischief."

—Foreword Reviews

"A ghost, a hidden treasure, and a race against time . . . Lisa Schmid's debut novel is a heartwarming mystery that belongs in the hands of every middle-school reader!"

—Lindsay Currie, author of *The Peculiar Incident on Shady Street*

"A fun, spooky mystery filled with humor and heart!"

—Jonathan Rosen, author of *Night of the Living Cuddle Bunnies*

"The search for gold brings history alive as Ollie searches for gold with his new best friend Teddy—who just happens to be a ghost!"

—Linda Joy Singleton, author of the Curious Cat Spy Club series

Ollie Oxley and the Ghost

THE SEARCH FOR LOST GOLD

Ollie Oxley and the Ghost

THE SEARCH FOR LOST GOLD

LISA SCHMID

JOLLY
FiSH
PRESS

ghts, Minnesota

First Edition
First Printing, 2019

Book design by Sarah Taplin
Cover design by Sarah Taplin
Cover illustrated by George Doutsiopoulos

Jolly Fish Press, an imprint of North Star Editions, Inc.

Library of Congress Cataloging-in-Publication Data (pending)
978-1-63163-289-1

Jolly Fish Press
North Star Editions, Inc.
2297 Waters Drive
Mendota Heights, MN 55120
www.jollyfishpress.com

Printed in the United States of America

For Oliver

CHAPTER 1
NEW HOUSE

Ollie Oxley squeezed his eyes shut, hoping the house might change from pink to blue or even a nice shade of green. He opened his eyes. Still pink. *Bummer.*

His black Labrador retriever rested his head on a tattered suitcase and whined. "It's okay, buddy." Ollie scratched Gus behind the ears. "We're here. Wherever here is."

"Drumroll please!" Ollie's mom thumped her hands on the steering wheel in rapid-fire succession. "Welcome to our new house!"

"It looks like an oversized dollhouse," Ollie said, crawling out of the back seat.

"It's a Victorian," Mom swooned, as if that justified its cotton-candy pink exterior.

"Yes. That makes it way better," Ollie deadpanned. "It's bad enough I'm the new kid. Now I am the new kid who lives in a Barbie Dreamhouse . . . Awesome."

"It's a pinkalicious delight!" Ollie's little sister sprang from the car and twirled up the driveway. "I can perform talent shows on the balcony."

"If your talent is 'annoying pest,' then you'll be amazing, Delilah." Ollie laughed, cracking himself up.

"You think you're so funny, but you're *snot*." She stuck her nose in the air and flipped her ponytail as she turned away. "For the last time, my stage name is DeeDee, spelled capital *D*, small *E-E*, capital *D*, small *E-E*."

"Whatever, drama queen. For the record, that's so dumb. Spelled capital *D-U-M-B*."

"Stop!" Mom held out her arm to block Ollie's way. "You know the rules. No one crosses the threshold until I roll out the red carpet."

"Oh, brother." He rolled his eyes. "This isn't a Broadway premiere."

"Don't be silly," Mom said, racing ahead to roll out the red *Welcome Home* mat. "Every day is a premiere."

"More like a bad movie," he muttered, unloading his suitcase from the car. Snapping the handle in place, he dragged the bag over the buckling sidewalk and up the stairs to the front door. "Can't we just be a normal family for once?"

"We *are* normal." Mom shook out the mat. A cloud of dust billowed into the air. "We're just a different kind of normal."

"Normal people don't move *all* the time." He blinked furiously, his hazel eyes watering from the dust.

Mom draped a reassuring arm around his sagging shoulders. "Sweetie, I'm tired of moving, too."

"Uh-huh." Ollie raked his fingers through his straw-colored

hair and zoned out on a black beetle as it scuttled across the porch. He watched until it disappeared beneath a stack of yellowing newspapers.

"This time it'll be different. I promise." Mom laid the *Welcome Home* mat at his feet. "The Bingham Theater has been here since I was a kid. It's not going anywhere, and neither are we. Can you just try and be happy?" she asked, digging through her purse for the house key.

Ollie nodded but stayed silent. He wanted to be happy. Really, he did. But ever since his dad left five years ago, everything had gone horribly wrong. His mom went back to work, which wasn't a bad thing, except now they moved every time she landed a new job directing some lame play or indie movie. They never stayed in one place for long, and he was always getting in trouble. He'd done more time in more principals' offices, than, well, most principals.

Moving sucked, but on the bright side, every new school came with a fresh new start.

Just then the beetle crawled out from under the newspapers and froze after getting hit with a spray of snot from DeeDee's fat pug, Hank.

I know how you feel, little dude. Somebody's always raining on my parade, too.

"Found it!" Mom cried, jingling a set of keys in the air. "Don't forget to wipe your feet on the red carpet for good luck." She jammed the key into the lock, turned the knob, and shoved hard with her shoulder. The door swung open with a slow, creaking moan as if to say "turn back now."

Ollie stepped *over* the red carpet and walked inside. A musty smell crept into his nostrils, followed by a whisper of cool air. He stood still for a moment, letting his eyes adjust to the gloomy interior. *Ugh!* He rubbed his eyes. *What. A. Dump.*

The walls were the color of scrambled eggs, which paired well with the old floorboards that resembled long strips of burnt bacon. Dusty cobwebs dangled from a crystal chandelier in the foyer and faded curtains swayed in the breeze that came in through a broken window. It was definitely a dump, but at least it was better than the last dump, or the dump before that, or the dump before that.

"Heads-up, Buttercup!" DeeDee pushed by him and bounded up the staircase with Hank hot on her heels. Moments later, she leaned over the banister and yelled, "I call dibs on both rooms up here!"

"What?" Ollie threw his hands up in the air. "Why should DeeDee get two rooms?"

Mom dropped the box of books she was carrying with a loud thud. Puffs of dirt swirled about her feet like mini tornados. "Sweetie, DeeDee could use the extra space for her costumes. There's a lovely room for you right here," she added, opening a door off the living room.

Ollie peered inside the cramped quarters. "You'd think the fact that I'm twelve and she's only ten might count for something, but I guess not." He sighed and lugged his suit-case into the tiny space. A pair of dust bunnies rolled across the floor like tumbleweeds.

The room—or lack of room—looked barely big enough, by his calculations, to fit his bed, his green dresser, and his red beanbag chair. A round window that reminded him of a ship's porthole looked out across the street at a yellow cottage with a white picket fence.

He crossed the room and pressed his face up against the glass. There was a sign painted on the weathered boards of the fence. "Miss Sally, World-Famous Medium," he read aloud. *Why does a world-famous medium live in a crummy little house on Peach Street?*

Before he could give it much thought, Gus padded into the room. His massive paws clicked on the hardwood floor. Butting his head up against Ollie's backside, he barked in loud, sharp bursts, nudging him toward the door.

"All right, buddy." Ollie chuckled. "Let's go check out your new digs."

Gus made a mad dash out of the room and down the hall, skidding to a halt when he reached the back door. Ollie rattled the glass doorknob back and forth. After a few stout tugs and a swift kick, the door jerked open, and Gus barreled by to find the closest tree.

Scrambling to get out of the way, Ollie banged into the doorjamb and nearly lost his balance. "Thanks a lot, Gus," he grumbled, scoping out the scenery. "Wow. This place is about as cheery as a graveyard."

The backyard hummed with summer insects that swarmed over a carpet of dandelions. Overgrown bushes and weeds had staged a hostile takeover of the garden. A series of old stepping-stones led to a small outhouse smothered in ivy.

The sprawling yard reminded him of an old cemetery he'd once visited while on a historical tour in New Orleans. *I hope that's not a mausoleum,* he thought, eyeing the outhouse. The above-ground burial chambers he'd seen on the trip had given him the willies. He half-expected a door to swing open and a zombie to creep out.

A white cat appeared from around the corner of the house and slinked through the tall grass. Gus sprang into action and chased the feline up a towering oak tree. The cat stared down from its perch with an amber gaze while Gus circled below, growling and scratching at the tree.

Ollie watched the commotion with amusement until something unusual caught his eye. A bent piece of metal was poking out from the trunk near the foot of the tree. The metal seemed to have grown with the tree, twisting and molding itself around the gnarled roots.

What the heck? He tramped through the weeds and knelt down to examine the object. Dead leaves and caked-on dirt encrusted the steel band. Using his fingernail, he chipped away at the muck until he uncovered letters etched into the metal. He ran his fingers over the engraving. A shiver ran down his spine. *Weird.*

Straining to get a better look in the fading sunlight, Ollie used the hem of his T-shirt to polish the metal. *W-A-L* was all he could make out. Reddish-brown rust obscured the last of the inscription.

"Movers are here!" DeeDee called from the house.

Ollie spat on his shirt and rubbed the metal one more time. "Coming," he mumbled but stayed focused on the rust that would not budge. Further investigation would have to wait. With one last curious glance over his shoulder, he went inside with Gus on his heels.

Two burly men from the Sedona Sands Moving Company were hauling their belongings into the house. It didn't take long. When Ollie's dad bolted, he took half of everything. All he'd left behind was one family, a faded plaid couch, matching overstuffed chair, an antique armoire, a beat-up coffee table, three sets of bedroom furniture, a chipped kitchen table with three chairs (Mom kicked the fourth to the curb), a couple dozen boxes, and a ginormous bookshelf that Mom absolutely refused to part with. When the movers were done, Mom signed a form, and they hustled out the door, anxious to get back on the road.

"Hey, Mom," Ollie said, as he dug through a cardboard box marked *Kitchen* in search of silverware and plates. "How old do you think this house is?" he asked, thinking about the metal in the oak tree.

Mom dumped a box of mac and cheese into a pot of boiling water. She slowly stirred the pasta as she pondered the question. "It's been here a long time," she said with a distant look in her eyes. "I visited here often when I was a kid. Your grammie was best friends with Dot—that's the lady who used to live here. And if I remember correctly, Grammie grew up coming here, too, so that would mean . . ."

"It's old!" DeeDee plopped down at the kitchen counter. "Like, really old."

Mom shook her head and chuckled. "Yes. Prehistoric. I'm pretty sure dinosaurs roamed the neighborhood."

Ollie set out three mismatched plates and plastic forks. "I didn't think it was that old. I betcha it's haunted," he speculated with a sideways glance at his sister.

"Mom!" DeeDee whined. "Do you think it's haunted?" Her eyes grew big and round. "I did hear strange noises upstairs."

"That was just your dog farting." Ollie snickered. "Stinky? Maybe. Scary? No."

"There's no such thing as ghosts." Mom gave Ollie the side-eye and scooped a blob of yellow mac and cheese onto each of their plates. "Now, eat."

Ollie ate his dinner in silence, still thinking about the mysterious piece of metal in the oak tree. What did the letters mean? *What words start with the letters W-A-L? Wallace? Walnut? Walrus? Definitely not walrus.*

Mom snapped her fingers in the air, pulling him out of his thoughts. "It's time for a toast."

"Oh, brother," he groaned. "Do we really have to?"

"Yes," Mom said. "We really have to."

DeeDee dramatically raised her paper cup filled to the brim with instant lemonade. "To our new house."

"To our new house," Mom echoed.

Ollie glanced down at his cup. It was half-empty. "To our new house." His voice sounded soft, even to himself.

Mom turned to Ollie, her blue eyes filled with concern. "You just need a good night's sleep." She gently ruffled his hair and gave him a kiss on the top of his head. "In the morning, everything will feel like new."

"It always does," he said in a near whisper.

A short time later, Ollie lay in bed with Gus curled up by his side. Maybe this time things would be different. Maybe this time they would stay put long enough for him to make a friend. Yawning, he pushed Gus to the foot of the bed and drifted off into a troubled sleep.

———

Ollie awoke with a start just past midnight. Moonlight streamed in through the window, casting eerie shadows on the wall. A sudden gust of wind shook the house and rattled his nerves. His heart skipped a beat. He pushed himself up onto one elbow, just enough to see out the window. The street lamp flickered off and back on, illuminating Miss Sally's house. On her porch swing there sat a boy.

With his arm draped casually across the back of the swing, the boy kicked his legs back and forth like he didn't have a care in the world. Even though it was a hot August night, he was wearing a long-sleeved white shirt and black pants with suspenders. He looked to be around twelve or thirteen, with shaggy blond hair and pale white skin.

What struck Ollie as strange—other than it being the dead of night—was that this boy looked vaguely familiar. Had they met before? Ollie sat up and leaned forward, craning his neck for a better view.

Suddenly, the boy stopped swinging and turned, staring intently at Ollie's window.

Can he see me? Ollie fell back and yanked the covers up over his head. The hairs on the back of his neck prickled. A split second later, he lowered the blanket and peered out the window.

The boy was gone.

CHAPTER 2

NEW TOWN

A high-pitched ring blared from the clock radio. Ollie sat bolt upright in bed and clobbered the OFF button. "What the—" His heart raced and his head buzzed with adrenaline. He looked around the room in confusion. It was his first morning in the new house, so it took a moment to make sense of his surroundings.

He blew out a deep breath of air and lay back down. Just before drifting off again, his eyes sprang open. *Porch Boy!* He jerked forward and stared out the window. Miss Sally's porch swing rocked gently in the breeze, but there was no boy in sight.

Gus stirred to life, lifted his head off the bed and gave it a good shake. Threads of slobber splattered the wall. With a burst of excitement, he jumped to all four paws and licked Ollie's face. At the same time, a low whistle sounded from the spot just below his tail.

"Aww, jeez, Gus," Ollie wheezed. "Farting—not cool." Holding his breath, Ollie leapt out of bed and raced out of the room to escape Gus's air biscuit. The welcoming aroma of chocolate-chip pancakes wafted through the air.

In the kitchen, DeeDee was sitting at the table, head down, studying a script. Hank was parked by her side with his pink tongue lolling out. At the sight of Gus, he jumped up and ran circles around him.

"Morning, sweetie." Mom greeted Ollie with a stack of pancakes. "Did you sleep well?"

"Yeah, I guess." Ollie sat down at the counter. "If you like sleeping in another new house in another new town."

Mom tucked a wisp of blonde hair behind her ear and rubbed the bridge of her nose. She drew a sharp breath and then released it before speaking. "Sweetie, Granite City isn't just any new town. I grew up here."

"I know, I know." Ollie reached for the pancakes. "Our ancestors were some of the first settlers. Blah. Blah. Blah."

In response, Mom flipped a pancake high into the air. It rotated twice before landing on the spatula in her outstretched hand. "Ta-da!" she trilled. "I bet our ancestors couldn't do that."

"Not unless they worked at IHOP," Ollie mused. Saturday morning pancakes were an Oxley family tradition, but not even chocolate-chip pancakes could cheer him up today. He grabbed the syrup bottle and painted a smiley face on his pancake. *Don't worry. Be happy.*

"I was thinking," Mom interrupted his epic pity party. "After we unpack, let's walk to town and check out the Bing. Then we can stop by Cook's Candy for ice cream."

"What's a Bing?" he asked, raising an eyebrow.

"The Bing is what we locals call the Bingham Theater." Mom poured him a glass of apple juice. "It has a nice ring to it. Don't ya think?"

"Speaking of a *not-so-nice* ring . . ." Ollie gave DeeDee his best bug-eyed stare. "Thanks a lot for turning on my alarm clock."

DeeDee lowered her script. "I didn't touch your stupid alarm clock."

"Riiight." He narrowed his eyes. "It just switched itself on."

DeeDee gasped and sprang to her feet. "You caught me!" She crouched, arms out, fingers splayed, eyes darting. "Late at night, I snuck into your room." She paused for effect. "It was then, and only then, that I realized you had nothing, and I mean *nothing*, that I wanted. So what's a burglar to do?" she asked, turning to her audience.

Ollie cocked his head and gave her the slow blink. "Gosh. I don't know."

Mom giggled.

"I did what any self-respecting burglar would do." She pounded the air with her fingers. "Dun-Dun-Dun-Dunnnn! I turned on your alarm clock!" Throwing her head back, she cackled. "Muah-ha-ha-ha-ha."

Ollie stared at her with a straight face and tried not to laugh. She was definitely annoying. But man, sometimes she really cracked him up. Like now. Finally, he gave way and chuckled. "Whatever."

Mom clapped her hands. "Bravo!"

DeeDee twirled her hand in the air and bowed. "Thank you. Thank you, very much. I'm here most evenings and weekends."

Still giggling, Mom started clearing plates. "I'm glad we got that settled." She tossed Ollie a wink and smiled. "Now, let's get to work."

———————

By the time they finished unpacking, the house almost felt like home. Almost. The furniture was in its proper place, the pictures were hung, and books were crammed into the bookshelf. Ollie kicked the last cardboard box in the living room to make sure it was empty. "All done!"

"Coming!" Mom called from down the hall.

Just then a flicker of movement caught his eye as the faded curtains billowed ever so slightly. Gus lifted his head off the rug and growled. Ollie crept forward, yanked the curtains to the side . . . and tumbled backward, landing with a thump on his rump, as a little mouse scurried across the floor.

Mom and DeeDee entered the room and waded through the sea of empty boxes. His sister came to a stop and peered down at him with a smug grin. "Mopping the floor with your butt?" Hank waddled over and licked his face.

"Yes. Yes, I am." Ollie wiped the slobber off his cheek, scrambled to his feet and brushed the dust off his shorts. "It's a dirty job, but someone's gotta do it. At least I'm making myself useful, which is more than I can say for you."

"At least I—"

"Enough!" Mom inspected the only box sitting upright. "What about this one?"

Gus circled the box and nudged it with his snout while Hank bounced up and down and yapped like a spider monkey.

Ollie frowned at the carton stuffed with family photos. "I could've sworn I unpacked that box." *Weird.* He rubbed the goosebumps on his arm and eyeballed the room.

"Never mind. We'll get it later." Mom pushed the box up against the wall. "Let's hit the road."

"Uh, yeah, let's get out of here." Ollie glanced over his shoulder at the box as if it might follow him out the door. Then he turned to Gus. "Easy, boy," he said, patting his dog on the head.

DeeDee plucked Hank off the ground and gave him a big smooch on his smashed-in face. "We'll be back soon, Mr. Hanky. Mommy loves you."

"Oh, brother." Ollie opened the door. "It's definitely time to go."

The trio set off to explore their new neighborhood. The smell of freshly cut grass hung in the air and a lawn mower hummed nearby. Huge oaks provided a tunnel of shade against the sweltering California sun.

They traveled west on Peach Street, hung a left on Apple Avenue, and followed the road past Victorian houses tucked behind white picket fences. In almost every yard, fruit trees dotted the lawns. Ripe peaches lay scattered on the ground like small, squishy balls.

Using DeeDee's Hello Kitty backpack as a moving target, Ollie amused himself with a bit of soccer practice. Taking aim, he gave one plump peach a good thwack. It shot through the air like a mushy missile and landed next to her on the sidewalk.

Splat!

"Oh . . . So close!" Ollie threw back his head and groaned.

As a diversionary tactic, Mom started to ramble on about local history like a Granite City tour guide. "Our neighborhood was originally a fruit orchard owned by a wealthy family in the 1800s. Over the years, the land was sold off piece by piece to build homes. But as you can see, many of the trees are still here." She swept her arms though the air in a panoramic gesture.

Even though Ollie found this mildly interesting, he was far more curious about Porch Boy. Who was this strange kid? And why was he up so late? "Hey Mom, do you know if Miss Sally has kids?"

"Gosh, Ollie." DeeDee's hands flew to her mouth in a

dramatic gasp. "Say it isn't so! Are ya gonna try and make a new friend?"

"Hi-larious." Ollie doubled over in fake laughter. "Maybe you should make like a clown and join the circus."

"Yeah. Well. Maybe you should make like a tree and leave."

"Yeah. Well. Maybe—"

"Seriously, enough!" Mom stopped abruptly and waited for Ollie to catch up. "No kids. Why?"

"Just curious. I saw a boy on her porch last night. One second he was there, then poof, he was gone."

"Aww. How sweet. Ollie has an imaginary friend," DeeDee teased. "Uh-oh. Maybe the Stuarts are back."

Ollie's face burned hot at the mention of the Stuarts—his ten imaginary friends—all named Stuart. When he was five, the Stuarts were his constant companions and partners in crime. When a fart filled the air, he'd plug his nose and cry, "Pee-ew! Bad Stuarts." When DeeDee's blankie went missing, he'd wag his finger and shout, "Naughty Stuarts, bring blankie back." Last, but not the least humiliating, at bedtime he'd insisted Mom kiss all ten Stuarts good night.

"You know, Ollie isn't the first person to have an imaginary friend," Mom said.

"Oh yeah?" DeeDee scoffed. "Who else has an imaginary friend?"

"As a matter of fact, Miss Sally did." Mom gave Ollie a conspiratorial wink.

Ollie's eyes widened. "She did?"

"Sure did. Come to think of it, Miss Sally was about your age when she first started talking about him."

"What happened?" He'd never known anyone—other than himself—who'd had an imaginary friend.

"Well, an imaginary friend when you're five is normal. Not so much when you're twelve. Kids nicknamed her *Spooky Spratt*." Mom shook her head. "To this day, she still swears by her imaginary friend. Sadly, I don't think she's ever really moved on."

"Really? 'Cause being a world-famous medium seems like she's totally moved on," Ollie remarked with a touch of sarcasm.

"World-famous medium or not, she's an old friend, so not another word. Anyway, we're here."

Country music filled the air from a band playing in the historic town center. The sidewalk bustled with people shopping and families out for a stroll. In a small café, guests dined under red umbrellas. The murmur of conversations blended with the tinkling of glass and the clattering of silverware. A giggling group of children wearing party hats jostled one another, and blew noise makers at a birthday boy. Balloons danced in the air and a half-eaten cake was sitting on the table. The boy's father snapped pictures from different angles, encouraging his son to smile for the camera. "Say cheese!"

A twinge of loneliness tugged at Ollie's gut. He missed his dad and he missed having friends.

Picking up the pace, he moved quickly past DeeDee, who'd stopped to admire her reflection in a window, and Mom, who'd paused to check her phone for messages. A couple of doors down, he came to a halt in front of the Granite City History Museum. He loved history, even earning an A in his world history class last year. According to the sign on the door, the stone structure was built in 1849. "Mom, can we check this place out?" he asked when his mom walked up.

"History museum?" DeeDee groaned. "Yuck."

"Absolutely!" Mom rummaged through her purse, pulled out her wallet, and paid the two-dollar admission fee for each of them.

Wanting to be alone, Ollie broke away from his family to sightsee on his own. He wandered through the maze of musty rooms, exploring the collection of Gold Rush artifacts and exhibits that chronicled the town's history. Hundreds of black-and-white photographs from the 1800s provided a glimpse back in time. He found it strange that not a single person in the old portraits was smiling. *Jeez. I thought I was bummed out.*

"Our museum was originally a Pony Express station," a friendly voice from behind him commented.

Ollie spun around to find a petite woman with a shock of white hair that reminded him of the end of a Q-tip. She was wearing a floor-length, blue gingham dress belted at the waist. Brown lace-up boots peeked out from under her skirt, and a leather satchel hung over her shoulder by a strap. His eyes flickered back and forth between the old photographs and the walking Q-tip. She looked like she'd just stepped out of one of the portraits—minus the grumpy face.

Placing her hands on her hips, she took a good look at Ollie. "You must be my new neighbor, Ollie Oxley. The name's Sally Spratt. But you may call me Miss Sally."

"Whoa! Did a ghost tell you I'd be here?" Ollie gaped in amazement. "You know . . . being that you're a medium."

"No visiting spirits today." Her green eyes sparkled. "I ran into your mom by the Sutter's Mill display. We had a nice time catching up."

"Are you like the museum manager?"

"I'm the curator. So, yes, I *am* the manager. I'm in charge of preserving Granite City history."

"It says here"—Ollie pointed to a bronze plaque on the wall—"that modern-day prospectors still find gold in Granite City. Is that true?"

"Yes. But it's very rare. You're more likely to unearth a secret stash of gold a prospector hid for safekeeping. That's if you know where to look."

His eyes grew big and round. "Do you know where to look?"

"No." Her lips puckered up as if she'd just sucked on a tart lemon. "I once spent an entire summer searching for gold. Much to my dismay, I never found anything but an old coin and a rusty key."

"How did ya know where to look then?"

"Let's just say I had inside information," she said, giving a small smile before her face flashed with irritation. "Albeit bad information."

What does she mean by inside information? Ollie wondered. "Well, let me know if you find any new clues. I love a good treasure hunt."

"Will do," she assured him. "How do you like your new house?"

Ollie frowned. "It's pink. Very—very pink."

"It most certainly is that," she agreed. "Years ago, your house was a bed and breakfast called the Tickled Pink Inn."

"That's cool." Ollie shrugged. *Cool . . . If you wanna be the new kid who lives in a pink house.* "But why pink?"

"Dot, the innkeeper, thought pink made people feel happy."

"Yeah, maybe if you're a girl." He tugged at his eyebrow and glanced away.

"It's more than just a pink house. It's one of the oldest homes in Granite City." Miss Sally dug through her leather satchel and pulled out a tri-fold brochure. "It's a historical landmark. See for yourself," she added, unfolding the handout.

"Awesome," he remarked dryly, staring at the grainy photograph of his house with the caption that read TICKLED PINK INN, BUILT 1857.

"It *is* awesome," Miss Sally gushed. "Here, take this with you." She handed him the brochure. "When you have a chance, you can read more about Granite City history."

As he stuffed the brochure into his back pocket, Ollie caught sight of Mom and DeeDee heading for the gift shop. "I should get going."

"Of course. I can rattle on for hours about Granite City. Let me know if you ever have any questions. I'm always happy to talk history."

"Thank you." Ollie touched his forehead in a casual salute and walked away. In the gift shop, he found Mom and DeeDee speaking to a museum employee.

"When gold was discovered in 1848, prospectors flocked to Granite City," the sales clerk was saying. "With a little luck and this gold pan, maybe you, too, can hit the mother lode."

"Mom, can we please go?" DeeDee stomped her foot and pointed toward the exit. "I want to see the Bing."

"In a minute." Mom turned to Ollie. "Sweetie, would you like a gold pan?"

"Sure." Ollie examined the metal pan. It looked like

Mom's Chinese wok, minus the handle. The exterior was smooth, but the interior had little ridges. "Who knows? Maybe I'll strike it rich."

Mom beamed. "I like your pioneer spirit!"

The sales clerk stuffed the gold pan into a brown paper bag with a Granite City History Museum logo stamped on the side and handed it to Ollie.

"Thanks, Mom," he said with a tight smile.

It's not like panning for gold was high on his to-do list, but at least it didn't sound life threatening or dangerous. Mom was always encouraging him to get involved in local activities. For Ollie, this meant surfing in Florida (jellyfish sting), horseback riding in Virginia (broken arm), hiking in Colorado (bear encounter), and mutton busting in Texas (ten stitches). Panning for gold sounded like a walk in the park.

What could possibly go wrong?

CHAPTER 3
NEW ENEMY

Ollie shot an uneasy glance up and down the street. "Are you sure this is the Bing?" he asked, feeling less than enthusiastic. "It looks like a run-down movie theater."

A gaudy sign jutted over the sidewalk—white lights blinked off and on in slow succession as if struggling to stay lit. Bits of plaster had crumbled away from the siding, leaving behind deep pockmarks. The art deco building may have been fancy at one time, but now it felt dingy and sad.

"It *is* the Bing!" DeeDee jumped up and down and clapped her hands like a circus seal on springs. "Look, Mom, there's a poster for *Chicago*. It even has your name on it."

"That's ironic, considering we lived in Chicago, like, three moves ago," Ollie muttered under his breath.

"It's locked," Mom said trying the door. "I need to get the keys from Captain Cook."

"Aww," DeeDee pouted.

"So sad." Ollie feigned disappointment. He did not share his family's love of show business. After all, that's what kept them on the move.

The Bing and Cook's Candy were in the same building,

and a black plaque with gold lettering posted on the wall between the two businesses read HISTORIC BINGHAM AND BEANS BUILDING. ESTABLISHED 1920. A cheery pink and white striped awning hovered above the Cook's Candy door and images of rainbow-colored lollipops were painted on the window.

"Before we go in, do you kids promise to behave?" Mom asked. "Captain Cook is my new boss and a childhood friend, so no horsing around."

The siblings nodded. But behind Mom's back, Ollie screwed up his face and crossed his eyes. DeeDee stuck her tongue out and made rude noises.

"Very nice. Is that what they teach you in drama class?" Ollie smirked as he nudged her out of the way and opened the door.

A bell chimed overhead. Inside the tiny shop, he caught a whiff of sugar and cinnamon. His mouth watered. Wood barrels stuffed with salt water taffy lined the wall and gold boxes of chocolates in all shapes and sizes decorated the shelves. *Sweet!* An old-fashioned, white ice cream freezer was calling his name. He could always count on a double scoop of rocky road to make him feel at home.

"Ahoy there," a deep voice came from the back room. "I'll be right with you."

Before long, a man appeared carrying a tray of freshly baked snickerdoodles. He looked like he couldn't decide what he wanted to be for Halloween—a pirate or a pastry chef. The bright red bandana tied around his head made his ears stick out, and his smile revealed a gold front tooth. He was wearing black-and-white checkered chef pants, and a white apron with a skull and crossbones stitched in black across the pocket.

"Well, shiver me timbers!" He set the tray down and came out from behind the counter to give Mom a big hug. "You're a sight for sore eyes, Jenny Oxley."

"Hey, Cookie." Mom hugged him back. "It seems like only yesterday we hung out while your dad did all the baking. How are you?"

"Life's sweet. Even sweeter now that you're back in town. Are you all settled into the house?" He winced. "Sorry. It's not exactly shipshape. No one's lived there since my Aunt Dot."

"It's perfect." Mom looped her arm through his and ushered him to her children. "I assume the kids still call you Captain Cook?"

"Arrrr!" He squinted one eye shut like a pirate. "And who are these fine buckos?"

"This is Ollie and DeeDee."

Ollie shook Captain Cook's hand. "Nice to meet you."

DeeDee curtsied then uttered in a dramatic tone, "Charmed, I'm sure."

"Ahoy, me hearties. It's good to meet you at long last." He grabbed a set of keys off a brass hook and handed them to Mom. "We've hit on hard times, lassie. I'm counting on you to bring the Bing back to life. It's nothing a sold-out season can't fix."

"I'll do my best," she replied. "Your offer came at the perfect time. When the last show wrapped, I wasn't sure where we'd go next."

"Aye." Captain Cook nodded. "Timing is everything."

While the grown-ups reminisced, Ollie scanned the rows of ice cream for rocky road. The bell chimed as more people entered the shop.

A chill that had nothing to do with ice cream filled the air.

Mom paused mid-sentence as if she'd seen a ghost.

Captain Cook's cheery smile faded into a straight line. "Son of a biscuit eater."

Oh, well. I might as well place my order. "Excuse me, Captain Cook, I'd like two—"

"Oi! Two scoops of rocky road in a plain cone," a girl demanded in a weird British accent.

"Hey!" Ollie cried.

Mom cut him off. "You know the rules, ladies first."

"But Mom, we were here first." Ollie glared at Rude Girl. She certainly did *not* look like a lady. She couldn't be much older than him, and judging by the sour look on her face, they were not going to be best friends. Her mouth sagged down in a frown, and her copper curls shot from her head like a blazing firecracker. Turning to Ollie, her eyes traveled him up and down and then slid away as if he wasn't up to snuff.

"Hello, Jenny. I just heard you were back in town," drawled a woman with dull red hair and a shiny red face. Deep frown lines framed her mouth as if she was always angry.

She must be Rude Girl's mom. Why doesn't she have a British accent?

"Hello, Edna," Mom replied in a frigid tone. "Kids, this is Mrs. Kelly. We grew up together."

"This is my daughter, Aubrey." Mrs. Kelly waved off Ollie and DeeDee with a quick flick of her hand. "She just got home from summer camp and couldn't wait to get an ice cream cone. Isn't that right, love bug?"

"Yes, Mummy," Aubrey cooed as she muscled past Ollie to grab her cone.

Love bug? Mummy? Gag! Ollie could feel his pancakes resurfacing. *Somebody's seen one too many Harry Potter movies.*

"So, Jenny." Mrs. Kelly leveled her gaze at Mom, "I hear you're staying at Dot Cook's old place. You know, they say it's haunted. Seen any ghosts, like our old pal Sally?"

"I'm not sure who *they* are, but whoever they are, they should really mind their own business," snapped Mom.

Aubrey leered at Ollie. "I say, will you be attending Suds?"

"Suds?" he asked, feeling about as dumb as they come.

"Don't be daft," Aubrey gurgled between slurps of her cone. "Sudbury Middle."

Rocky road ice cream framed her mouth. Ollie stifled a giggle and focused on the mole above her right eye that looked like a giant tick, ready to dive-bomb her nose.

"If you are, hopefully, you don't get Miller for homeroom. He's a bloody bore."

"I'm going to Sudbury. I mean Suds," he stammered, sincerely hoping they would not be in the same class. "I'm in the seventh grade."

"I, too, will be in the seventh grade. My mum's the PTA president, so I have clout, if you know what I mean."

"Yeah. Well, I'm going into fifth grade at Folsom Lake Elementary," DeeDee chimed in. "I, too, will have clout once I land the lead in the school play."

"Blimey." Aubrey yawned. "Isn't that special?"

"Why, thank you, milady." DeeDee bowed her head, not picking up on Aubrey's sarcasm. "Acting is a noble calling. Not everyone appreciates how truly special I am," she added, mean-mugging her brother.

Ollie cringed. *Why don't sisters come with an OFF switch?*

"Edna, I assume you still live in the neighborhood, so we'll see you around," Mom said, dismissing Mrs. Kelly. "All right, kids, let's place our order so Captain Cook can get back to work."

"A scoop of rainbow sherbet in a plain cone." DeeDee smiled sweetly.

"With pleasure, lassie." Captain Cook scooped her order and handed it to DeeDee. He turned to Ollie. "Now, laddie, what may I get for you?"

"Two scoops of rocky road in a chocolate waffle cone."

"Aarrgh," Captain Cook groaned. "Aubrey got the last of the rocky road. Do you have a second choice?"

His shoulders slumped. "A scoop of vanilla," Ollie muttered, disappointed.

Before leaving, Mrs. Kelly gave a parting shot to Captain Cook with a smug look of triumph. "You should have accepted the offer I sent last week. Sooner or later, the Bingham and Beans will be mine." Grabbing her daughter by the arm, she pushed the door open with a loud *bang*.

On her way out the door, Aubrey locked eyes with Ollie and smirked. "See ya, new kid."

Ignoring Mrs. Kelly, Captain Cook handed Ollie his cone. "Vanilla has always been my favorite. It's pure and simple goodness."

"Thank you, Captain—"

An earsplitting shriek pierced the air. Ollie whipped around just in time to see Aubrey take a spill onto the sidewalk. A moment later she reappeared with ice cream plastered on her face and dripping down the front of her blouse.

Porch Boy was outside leaning against a wood post,

thumbs hooked on his suspenders. A mischievous grin stretched across his face.

He waved at Ollie.

Ollie flashed a broad smile and waved back.

Aubrey glanced around wide-eyed and furious. Her face burned so red she looked like a Maraschino cherry dipped in chocolate sauce. Just then, she caught sight of Ollie gawking and grinning. Her lips parted in surprise and then pinched together in anger. Without so much as a glance in Porch Boy's direction, she stormed off in a huff.

Porch Boy shrugged as if to say "oh, well."

Ollie lowered his face and smacked his forehead. *Crap! It looks like I've made a new enemy.* When he looked up, Porch Boy was gone.

CHAPTER 4
NEW KID

Ollie hit the snooze button for the third time. No use in putting it off any longer. It was D-Day. His eyes fluttered open. The numbers on the clock radio glowed 7:15. He had thirty minutes to get dressed and ready for school. Swatting the OFF button, he crawled out of bed.

"I wish I could hang here with you, Gus," Ollie said as he threw on a pair of shorts, a T-shirt, a green sock, a blue sock, and black Converse sneakers. He never wore matching socks, mostly because he could never find a matching set. He was always losing things, including socks.

With a heavy sigh, he exited his room, shuffled down the hall, and tried to muster a smile before rounding the corner into the kitchen where DeeDee and his mom were eating breakfast. Gus trailed after him thumping his tail from side to side.

"Why so glum, chum?" DeeDee mumbled between bites of cereal.

Ollie drew back and wiped a speck of Froot Loops off his cheek. "Say it. Don't spray it."

Hank scrambled underfoot to snap up food droppings.

"Morning, sweetie. Ready for your first day?" Mom sounded a bit too chipper.

"Ready as I'll ever be." He grabbed a piece of toast and stuffed it into his mouth before trudging out of the kitchen and down the hall.

"Later, gator," DeeDee called out. "Try not to be such a Doogie Downer."

Mom traipsed after him, flicking imaginary lint off his shoulder and smoothing down his unruly hair. Ollie ducked and pulled away. "I'm not five."

"Sorry." Mom gave him a tight squeeze and planted a kiss on his head. "You got this."

"Mmm-hmm." Ollie gulped down the last bite of toast and hoisted on his backpack. "See ya tonight." He shoved his phone into his front pocket and then, for Mom's sake, he forced a grin and gave a double thumbs-up before heading out the door.

"Don't forget," Mom shouted after him. "Straight down Peach, then take a right on Orange Blossom."

"I know, I know," he said with a backward flip of his hand.

From down the street, he spotted a pack of kids coming his way. He shot a wary glance over his shoulder at the pink house. *So embarrassing.* Diving behind a flowery hedge, he waited for them to pass. A moment later, he bounced back up, opened the gate, and looked both ways. It was all clear, so he adjusted his backpack and headed to school.

Soon a few kids fell in step with him. He overheard snippets of conversations about shared summer vacations and birthday parties. The familiar pang of loneliness settled into his gut, like a three-day-old bean burrito. Slowing down to let them pass, he mentally shifted gears to Porch Boy. Did he go to Suds? Would they be friends?

Three short blocks later, he arrived at school just in time for the first bell. In the parking lot, he spied the only person he knew—Aubrey. She was hanging out in the shade of a peach tree, flanked by two stoic girls with steely stares. Neither girl flinched when Aubrey slugged some poor kid in the arm. Like stone gargoyles guarding a museum, their expressions remained cold and impassive.

"Hey!" the boy cried, rubbing his arm.

"I'll take that." Aubrey snagged his chocolate milk and cracked it open. She took a giant swig, then set her sights on Ollie. "Oi! Oxley! Hey, new kid, I'm talking to you."

Oh, brother. Ollie knew a bully when he saw one. They were all the same. Mean and dumb. By the tone of her voice, this would not be good. "Hey, Aubrey," he greeted her with a slight upward tilt of his chin.

"Don't 'hey' me." She glared at Ollie and her lip curled. "I saw you laughing at me the other day when I fell. I won't forget that anytime soon."

"I wasn't—"

"Shut it," she snarled. "I saw what I saw. By the way, this is Cinda and Sierra. They're my BFFNs."

"BFFNs?"

"Best Friends For Now," she explained. "If they don't follow the rules, things can change just like that." She snapped her fingers under his nose.

"Oh boy." He rolled his eyes. "Lucky them."

"Indeed." She paused to glare. "As I was saying, we rule the school, so stay out of our way. And another thing—"

Bonk!

A large peach fell from above and bounced off her head. "Aahh!" She tottered backward and tripped over the curb. Her arms flailed and her feet flew skyward—an orange flip-flop whizzed by Ollie's head. Chocolate milk rained down on her face and white blouse. That peach had stopped what had promised to be a most unpleasant speech.

"Hello!" Ollie snorted with mirth. "You can't seem to keep your feet on the ground and food off your face."

Aubrey grabbed Sierra by the arm and hoisted herself up. Her face flushed a raging red, making her look like an angry tomato. Kids slowed to a snail's pace and gawked like rubberneckers at a traffic accident. Nobody made a sound except for one unseen boy, whose giggles broke the silence.

"Stay out of my way, Oxley!" She swiped her chin with the back of her hand and flared her nostrils. While spewing a variety of curse words, she stuffed her feet back into her flip-flops and stomped away with her gargoyles in tow.

"Crap." *This has got to be a new record. I've pissed off the school jerkface before first period.* Ollie's shoulders drooped. *At least one kid laughed at my joke,* he thought, trying to focus on the bright side.

CHAPTER 5

NEW SCHEDULE

A couple of wrong turns later, Ollie found homeroom. *Showtime!* With his heart in his throat, he pulled the door open and stepped inside. The room buzzed with giddy chatter and the opening and closing of desk tops.

Mr. Miller sat in his chair with his feet kicked up on the desk, reading a copy of *Eat Green* magazine. Without bothering to look up, he greeted students between bites of apple. "Bell's about to ring. Take a seat."

Ollie surveyed the room for an empty desk. Aubrey and the gargoyles were sitting three rows back. *Really?* The day had barely begun, and it already felt like it would never end.

"Excuse me." A dark-skinned boy with a mop of brown hair bumped into him. "Coming through," he added, bee-lining his way to an open desk.

Now only two desks sat empty. One desk was directly behind Aubrey, the other was front row center. *No brainer.* Ollie hustled to the front of the class and slid into the empty chair. He pulled his *Health and Wellness* textbook from his backpack and thumbed idly through the pages. Casually, he snuck a peek over his shoulder. Much to his surprise, Porch Boy was now sitting at the desk behind Aubrey.

He waved at Ollie.

Hesitant, Ollie waved back.

Aubrey's eyes bugged out. She swiveled in her chair then turned back again to face Ollie. "You're crazy," she mouthed, twirling her finger next to her ear.

Porch Boy shrugged his shoulders and grinned.

Jeez. Aubrey acts like this kid doesn't exist. Lucky guy.

———————————

Forty-two excruciating minutes passed before Ollie's heart stopped racing. It felt like a pack of hamsters were tag-team wrestling in his chest. This was not how he pictured his first day. He could practically feel Aubrey burning a hole in the back of his head. The loud ringing of the bell jarred him out of his anxiety-riddled daze.

"Make healthy choices!" Mr. Miller shouted above the clatter of chairs.

Ollie stood up and shouldered his backpack. Even though he had a ten-minute break before second period, he wanted to get a move on. He snatched a look over his shoulder. Aubrey was pushing her way to the front of the class, her eyes laser focused on him.

"Loser," she hissed as she slithered by him.

Gritting his teeth, Ollie followed the rest of the herd out the door and down the corridor. Throngs of students spilled out from four sets of double doors and converged onto the quad, shuffling up the sidewalk with their heads down, eyes glued to their phones.

Feeling out of sorts and alone, he stopped at the water fountain to get a drink. While gulping down water, he scanned his surroundings with a well-trained eye.

Four two-story brick buildings surrounded the grassy area, and a sidewalk in the shape of a tic-tac-toe grid divided the quad. The middle square served as the social epicenter for the popular kids. Small clusters of students lingered in the surrounding squares like planets orbiting the sun.

A row of geeks sat with their backs against the library wall, burying their noses in books, and gamers huddled in circles, tapping away at their phones. It was the same at every school; all cliques had their go-to spot.

In the farthest corner, Aubrey held court with the gargoyles and a small entourage of suck-ups and wannabes. On cue, all eyes turned toward Ollie, followed by a spontaneous burst of guttural laughter.

His cheeks burned hot with anger. Clenching his fists, he wanted to scream, "Leave me alone!" But he didn't. As the perpetual new kid, he was experienced in the art of bully warfare. Taking a deep breath, he mentally reviewed his rules of engagement.

1. When confronted by the enemy, employ evasive maneuvers.

2. Never let them see you sweat.

3. If rules one and two fail, run for your life.

Ollie rubbed his sweaty palms against his shorts then went on to implement rule number one. He made his way across the quad in search of a place to escape the village idiots. Next to the multipurpose room, he found an empty spot at a picnic table in the shade of a giant oak tree. *Perfect!* After settling in on the bench, he pulled out his new schedule.

1st Period: Health and Wellness – Miller / Room 10

2nd Period: Pre-Algebra – Moran / Room 4

3rd Period: Language Arts – Arguelles / Room 18 Lunch

4th Period: Science – Cruz / Room 22

5th Period: P.E. – Adler / Gymnasium

6th Period: Geography – Barnett / Room 6

7th Period: Spanish – Barajas / Room 25

Please don't have the same schedule as Aubrey, Ollie silently prayed to the middle school gods. A sudden gust of wind blew a shower of leaves across the grass, lifting his schedule off the table. He slapped the paper down before it could take flight.

"What a butthead," said a cheerful voice in front of him.

Ollie's head jerked up. "Excuse me?"

Porch Boy leaned against the oak tree with his thumbs hooked on his suspenders. A smile danced across his lips. "Aubrey. Biggest butthead of all time."

Ollie eyed him with startled interest. Where the heck did

he come from? And why was he always wearing the same clothes? His shirt and pants were plain and old-fashioned. Not to mention the suspenders. *Who wears suspenders?*

"Name's Theodore, but you can call me Teddy," the boy said.

"Name's Oliver, but you can call me Ollie. All my friends do." Not that he had any, but it sounded good. "She really is a butthead," he agreed with a grim twist of his mouth.

"That's why pranking her is so much fun." Teddy chuckled. "When she gets mad, her face practically implodes. Especially when it's covered with chocolate milk."

"Can you believe she got peach-bombed?" Ollie marveled. "What are the odds?"

"I'd say about two to one. " Teddy gave a sly grin.

What's that supposed to mean? Ollie wondered. "By the way, what's up with her weird accent?"

"Dunno. Last summer she visited England for a month and came back with an accent. Go figure."

Ollie rolled his eyes. "Lame."

"Speaking of lame, here comes Aubrey with her side-kicks, Ding and Dong."

Like a swarm of angry bees, Aubrey and her entourage buzzed through the quad. Ollie watched in dismay as Aubrey shoulder-checked a girl into Cinda. "Hey!" Cinda shoved her roughly away. "Watch where you're going." The girl stumbled, regained her composure, wrapped her arms around her waist, lowered her head, and quickly moved away.

The yard duty lady did nothing. She yawned and looked the other way. Swinging the whistle that hung around her neck in circles, she disappeared in a crowd of students.

I guess that's what Aubrey meant by clout. Ollie cringed with sympathy. Turning his attention back to Teddy, he asked, "What's her problem, anyway? In class, she acted like you don't exist."

"To her, I don't. Never have," Teddy stated, matter-of-factly.

"That's kinda harsh. What'd ya do to piss her off . . . other than breathe the same air?"

A slow smile spread across Teddy's face, creating dimples in his freckled cheeks. "Honestly, I didn't even do that."

Ollie bristled. Something about Teddy seemed odd. His new-kid sense was tingling. "Didn't. Do. What?" he asked with a slight edge to his voice.

Teddy winced and rubbed his cheek. "Now, I can see you're getting all higgledy-piggledy, so I'll just catch up with you later.

"Higgledy-piggledy?" Ollie stared at him, dumbfounded. "What are you, eighty?"

Teddy stuck up his thumb and jerked it skyward. "Higher."

"What do you mean higher?"

"Look!" Aubrey shouted from across the quad. "The new kid's talking to himself."

Ollie gave Teddy the hairy-eyeball. "What the heck is going on?"

"Well . . ." Teddy's voice faltered. "There's never a good time to say this, so I'm just going to say it. I have good news and bad news."

Is this a riddle? Ollie tugged at his eyebrow.

"First, the good news. I'd like to be your friend."

That's a first. Ollie kept listening. Out of the corner of his eye, he could see Aubrey and the gargoyles rapidly approaching.

"Oi! Oxley! Don't be so bloody rude. Introduce us to your mate so we can all say hi," Aubrey said with a mocking sneer.

Teddy continued. "The bad news is, well, I'm a ghost." With a wink and a smile, he was gone. Not walk-away gone, but vanish-into-thin-air gone.

Ollie stared at the spot where Teddy had just been standing, mouth agape. "What the—" His stomach clenched and his brain ping-ponged around inside his head. The quad spun like a Tilt-A-Whirl. *I think I'm gonna barf.*

Kids around him hummed with excitement. He was the first social roadkill of the school year. Aubrey and the gargoyles formed a semi-circle, blocking his escape from his seat on the bench. "Hey, weirdo." Aubrey put her hands on her knees and leaned into his face. "I said introduce us to your mate."

Ollie met her gaze but remained silent. His mind was

swirling with questions. What just happened? Was this some kind of joke?

Cinda made a big show of looking under the picnic table. "Nobody here."

Sierra poked her head around the trunk of the tree. "Nobody here, either."

"Well, well." Aubrey snickered. "It looks like the new kid has an imaginary friend."

Ollie buried his face in his hands. *I'm losing it!* One second, he was having a perfectly normal conversation, which didn't happen every day. Then, wham bam, his new pal disappeared. Maybe the stress of so many moves had finally taken its toll. He'd read about post-traumatic stress syndrome in health class last year. Was this happening to him? *I'm only twelve!*

The second bell rang. For the moment, he was safe. Unfortunately, he was also late for class.

CHAPTER 6
NEW PENCIL

Ollie shaded his eyes and gazed upward at the sign on the building. Folsom Hall. *Wrong building.* He studied the school map printed on the reverse side of his class schedule. *Wait a minute.* He flipped it around. *Duh.* He trekked back across the quad, past the cafeteria, to Kelly Hall. He reached for the doorknob, but before he could turn it, the yard duty lady blocked his way.

"You're late," she said, eyeing him with disapproval.

"I got lost," he replied, unable to think of a better excuse. *You try making it to class on time when you're chitchatting with a ghost,* he thought to himself, not brave enough to say it aloud.

She snatched the schedule from his hand and read it. "Follow me." She handed back the crumpled piece of paper.

"Yes, ma'am." He stuffed the schedule into his front pocket, followed her through the door and then scampered down the hall after her. For a wiry old bird, she was quick on her feet.

At the end of the corridor, she came to a halt in front of room four. "This is you." She gave him one final disapproving look, then turned on her heel and strode off as if she had something far more important to do.

Ollie peered through the narrow window in the door. The teacher was perched on the edge of her desk. Her long, brown hair was pulled back in a ponytail and she was wearing an emerald-green jumpsuit with pointy black boots. He giggled. *My math teacher is an Elf on the Shelf.* But his jovial mood quickly evaporated at the sight of Aubrey and the gargoyles sitting in the back row. Aubrey ripped a page out of her binder and passed it to Cinda, who read it, shook with laughter, then gave it to Sierra.

Ollie had a sinking feeling. *That can't be good.* Squaring his shoulders, he assumed his best don't-mess-with-me face and swaggered into the room. Thirty pairs of eyeballs sized him up. A low rumble of whispers picked up steam like an oncoming locomotive.

"Settle, people," instructed Miss Moran. "You must be Oliver Oxley." She referred to her roll call sheet. "It's your first day, so I'll give you a break. Take a seat."

Ollie squeezed through a row of desks to the only vacant seat in the middle of the room. A few random snickers broke the awkward silence that followed him. He collapsed into the chair and clutched his backpack to his chest. His face was hot and his ears were ringing.

The girl who sat behind Ollie tapped him on the back.

When he turned, she handed him a note. "This is for you," she whispered.

Ollie shifted uncomfortably in his seat, unfolded the paper, and read the message.

> Ollie Opley has a new friend.
> Imaginary to the end.
> If only we could see him, too.
> But clearly, Ollie has no clue.
> Making up a friend is sad.
> Things really do look bad.
> I heard a rumor and it's funny.
> His new friend is the Easter Bunny.

That's just dumb, Ollie thought to himself. *Is that the best she can do?* He had to admit, though, on short notice it wasn't too bad. At least this new bully could spell. The last bully could barely spell his *own* name.

———————

Ollie made it to last period with only seconds to spare. Out of breath, he pushed the door open and stumbled into class. A handful of students stopped talking and turned to gawk, scrutinizing him from head to toe.

"Hey." He gave a halfhearted wave and a lopsided grin. A couple of girls giggled, then went back to gossiping. *Probably discussing my morning display of crazy on the quad.* His gaze swept the room. There was no sign of Aubrey and the gargoyles. *Finally!*

Breathing a sigh of relief, he slid into a chair and dropped his backpack on the ground. *Be cool.* All day long he'd been trying to convince himself that he wasn't losing his mind. *There's no such thing as ghosts.* Maybe it was some kind of twisted hazing ritual that students played on the new kid using special effects like they do in the movies. There had to be a logical explanation. He eyed the room, searching the faces of his classmates for answers. Were they in on the joke?

Before class started, he checked his phone for messages. Nada. Then a thought crossed his mind. Flicking his finger across the screen, he switched over to the browser and Googled "Granite City ghosts." *Whoa!* There were over 345,000 results. The first couple of pages listed stories about ghosts of the Gold Rush and spooky sightings. Apparently his new town was a paranormal hotspot. *Maybe I'm not crazy after all.* He turned his phone off and dropped it into his backpack.

Trying his best to look cool, he stretched out his legs, interlaced his fingers atop his head, and waited for class to begin. Spanish was his favorite subject. He found it highly useful when ripping on DeeDee in front of Mom. DeeDee knew just enough Spanish to catch his drift.

The Spanish teacher stood up from her desk and walked up to the whiteboard. She cleared her throat. The din of student chatter quieted down. "Buenos días, alumnos. Soy la señora Barajas," she said, writing her name with a green dry-erase marker.

Ollie sat up straight, lifted the pencil from behind his ear and opened his spiral notebook. Tilting his head back, he balanced the #2 pencil between his lip and his nose.

"Esta es la clase de español." Señora Barajas turned around to face the class. "This year, plan on—"

The door opened and into the room stepped Aubrey.

"Ay, caramba," Ollie muttered and dropped his head forward. The pencil slipped off his lip, bounced off the desk and landed on the floor at Aubrey's feet. His heart sank like an anchor, and his shoulders slumped. *Perfecto.*

"Buenos días, señora Barajas." Aubrey crunched down on the pencil. With a quick backward flick of her foot, she sent it spiraling across the floor. "Lo siento por llegar tarde."

Ollie tracked the pencil's trajectory as it rolled across the tiles until it disappeared beneath the bookcase and out of reach. *I guess I need a new pencil*, he thought, reaching for his backpack.

"Nice Spanish." Señora Barajas arched an eyebrow at Aubrey. "However, I'd be more impressed if you made it to class on time. Sit, por favor. As I was saying . . ."

Aubrey sauntered over to the empty desk next to Ollie. "Hola, loser. Is this seat taken?"

Ollie glowered at her with the same wide-eyed, mildly

irritated expression he typically reserved for DeeDee. "Does it look taken?"

"I don't know. You tell me." She made a pouty face as if talking to a small child. "Is your wittle fwiend sitting here?"

The muscles tensed in his jaw and his eyes narrowed. "As a matter of fact, he is, and he thinks you're a complete butthead."

Several kids snickered. Aubrey's face went slack like a mushy bowl of oatmeal. Crimson stains appeared on each cheek. She pressed forward until she was inches from his nose. Foul breath—worse than Gus's on a bad day—blasted him in the face. "Just remember, I always get the last laugh."

"Ahem." Señora Barajas stood in front of the whiteboard, poised to write. "Is there a problem?"

"No problemo." Aubrey slid into the seat next to Ollie. "Just saying hola to the new kid."

The last bell finally rang, officially ending a less-than-spectacular start at a new school. Ollie shouldered his way through the crowded corridor. *Could this day get any worse?* He scoured the mass of kids pouring onto the quad. There was no sign of Aubrey, but that didn't mean she wasn't lurking nearby. He hunched his shoulders and headed up the sidewalk.

"Hey, Ollie, wait up," yelled someone from down the hall.

It was the boy he bumped into in homeroom. He tried to

remember the kid's name from first-period roll call, Gurdeep something or other. "If you're delivering a note for Aubrey, no thank you." Ollie rubbed his forehead. "I've already had my share of headaches today."

"No note. I promise." Gurdeep held both palms up to prove his hands were empty. "Aubrey and I aren't exactly friends." He lowered his voice to a whisper. "She's a jerk. In the fourth grade, she stole my lunch money. Every. Day."

"You went a whole year without lunch?"

"Almost. One time I hid it in my sock because it was Taco Tuesday."

"Ouch." Ollie frowned. "Why didn't you stand up to her?"

"Easier said than done. She punched me in the gut and called me a slacker," Gurdeep said, shuffling his feet. "But I got my taco," he added with a goofy grin.

"Seriously, dude, why didn't you hit her back?"

"My dad would kick my butt if I ever hit a girl. Besides," Gurdeep continued, splotches of red dappling his cheeks, "she's bigger than me."

"True." Ollie nodded. "So, what's up?"

"Well, it seems like you're not afraid of her. Like this morning in front of the school, you kinda stood up to her."

"I'm not sure cracking a lame joke is standing up to her." Ollie shrugged. "But if you say so."

"Here's the deal." Gurdeep's eyes darted around the quad.

"Aubrey's running for class president. So, some of us were talking and thought maybe you should run against her."

"What?" Ollie exclaimed. "Why would I do that?"

"Nobody else wants to." Gurdeep spat the words out as if they tasted as yucky as they sounded.

"Uh-huh, and your selling point is?" Ollie scowled.

"Rumor has it you move all the time. Win or lose; you're probably outta here. No harm, no foul, on to the next school. But if you win—that'd be epic."

"Nice." Ollie's eyes narrowed; annoyed disbelief wallpapered his face. "I'll take it into consideration."

Out of nowhere, Aubrey appeared like a not-so-silent-but-deadly fart, smoldering and unwelcome. "Hey, Gur-Dweep," she taunted in a sing-song baby voice. Sniggering, she shoulder-checked him hard and swaggered by with a sinister sneer.

"Gur-Dweep?" Ollie let out a low whistle and laid a sympathetic hand on his arm. "Dude, that's harsh."

"I know." His face crumpled like a used Kleenex. "It's so embarrassing."

Aubrey and the gargoyles flipped a U-turn at the end of the hall.

"Oh, brother." Ollie moved slightly forward, shifting his weight to his right foot to block Gurdeep. "Here she comes again."

"Oi! Oxley." Aubrey tilted her chin upward, eyes flashing with a challenge.

He met her gaze without flinching. "What do you want?"

"What I want, is for you to be gone," she replied with a nasty grin. "And, lucky for me, I always get my way."

"What's that supposed to mean?"

"It means you're outta here." Aubrey pulled up a message on her phone and then shoved it in his face. "According to my mom, Cook is about to lose his building. Unless he strikes it rich, you and your wacky family are history. Like I said, I always get the last laugh."

A wave of nausea washed over him. For the first time in his life, he had no snarky comeback.

CHAPTER 7
NEW FRIEND

Ollie stopped at the Forty-Niner Food Mart on his way home to buy a soda and chips. Maybe a salty snack would help clear his head. Munching on potato chips, he wandered down to the river and followed the trail until he came upon an old truss bridge with a sign posted at the entrance.

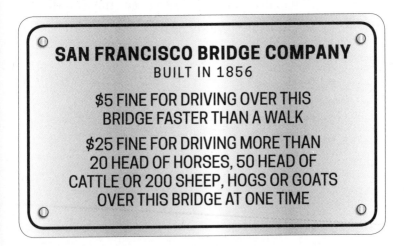

SAN FRANCISCO BRIDGE COMPANY
BUILT IN 1856

$5 FINE FOR DRIVING OVER THIS
BRIDGE FASTER THAN A WALK

$25 FINE FOR DRIVING MORE THAN
20 HEAD OF HORSES, 50 HEAD OF
CATTLE OR 200 SHEEP, HOGS OR GOATS
OVER THIS BRIDGE AT ONE TIME

The wood planks creaked beneath Ollie's feet as he made his way across the rustic bridge. He propped his elbows up on the railing and watched kayakers battling the rapids. Giant oak trees along the shore cast shadows on the river.

A bit farther upstream, raging waters cascaded over large boulders, creating little rock islands and swirling eddies.

"I remember when they built this bridge." Teddy sighed. "It ruined my favorite fishing hole."

"What the—" Ollie jumped like popcorn on a hot oiled pan. "Aww, jeez. Really? You're back?"

"You're a jittery little thing." Teddy eyed him up and down. "You should cut back on the soda pop."

"Whatever. Go haunt Aubrey and the gargoyles."

"Way ahead of you. No one deserves a good scare more than Aubrey, Tricky, and Dicky." Teddy chuckled. "Lucky for you, I want to be your friend."

"Lucky me," Ollie said, feeling anything but. Taking a step back, he sized up his new friend. He looked so real, not hazy and see-through like in the movies. "Are you really a ghost?"

"Cross my heart and hope to die," Teddy said, crisscrossing his heart.

Ollie raised one dubious eyebrow. "Prove it."

"Snippity-snap," Teddy murmured. "Somebody's got trust issues, and it ain't me." In a flash he vanished, then reappeared, sitting atop the railing and grinning from ear to ear. "Told ya I was a ghost."

"Awesome," Ollie muttered under his breath. "Just what every new kid needs, an invisible friend." For the first time, he noticed Teddy's bare feet. "I guess you didn't die with your boots on."

"Boots?" Teddy's head flinched back. "Why would I be wearing boots? That's an odd thing to say."

"You know, the joke: Why did the cowboy die with his boots on?"

"Dunno." Teddy shrugged. "Why?"

"'Cause he didn't want to stub his toe when he kicked the bucket." Ollie chuckled.

"Wow, you really know how to hurt a guy." Teddy lifted his right foot and wriggled it in the air. "I suppose that's how I stubbed my big toe."

Ollie eyed Teddy's bloody toe and wrinkled his nose. It looked like he'd stubbed it only yesterday. "Sorry about that. I guess it's not all that funny, considering."

"Aww, shucks." Teddy waved him off. "I'm just messing with you. My sense of humor didn't die with me."

"Good to know. There's nothing worse than a ghost who can't take a joke." Ollie glanced from side to side to make sure the coast was clear. "Anyway, what's the deal? Do you have unresolved issues? Afterlife got you down? If you're looking for a boost into the light, I'm not your guy."

"No boost." Teddy jumped off the railing and hooked his thumbs onto his suspenders. "It's just when I realized you could see me, I got excited. It's been years since I've talked to anyone."

"That's nice. Glad I could fill a void in your life—ghostly or otherwise."

"So I was thinking," Teddy continued. "I heard your conversation with Gurdeep, about running for class president. I say we do it. I can be your campaign manager."

Ollie quirked an eyebrow and frowned. "Yeah, that seems like a reasonable plan. Run for class president at a school where I have no friends, with a ghost as my campaign manager. How can I say no? You're not only dead, you're stone-cold crazy."

"No, seriously. Who better to help than a ghost? I can listen in on Aubrey's campaign meetings, undermine her efforts, and basically wreak spiritual havoc."

"Look, ghost dude, I've got enough problems of my own." Ollie's eyes flashed. "I'm *not* running for class president."

"Problems? What kind of problems?"

"Well, for one"—Ollie held up his thumb—"I've got a ghost stalking me." He paused and stared meaningfully at Teddy.

"I think that's a bit harsh," Teddy mumbled under his breath. "But go on."

"Two." Ollie held up his thumb and his index finger. "In case you haven't noticed, señorita Psycho has it out for me, and three . . ." He held up another finger. "It looks like I'm gonna have to move—again!"

"Move?" Teddy screwed up his face in confusion. "You just got here."

"Story of my life." Ollie kicked the railing post in frustration. Wood debris and dust mushroomed into the air.

Teddy scratched the side of his head. "I don't understand."

"I guess when you were eavesdropping, you didn't hear what Aubrey said." Ollie sighed. "Captain Cook is about to lose his building to the bank, which means my mom is about to lose her job, which means I'm outta here. Unless Cook strikes it rich, it's adiós, Granite City! Adiós, weird ghost."

The enormity of Ollie's dilemma finally registered on Teddy's face. He combed his fingers through his unkempt hair and gazed out at the water. "How long have you got?"

"Don't know. But it sounds like Captain Cook doesn't have much time."

Teddy bounced from foot to foot. "I think I can help."

"Really?" Ollie scoffed. "What exactly are you gonna do? Yell 'boo' at the bank?"

"Crackers and crawfish, you're an annoying cuss," Teddy scolded. "No. You and I are gonna partner up and find my pa's gold."

"Find your *pa's* gold?" Ollie replied, dumbfounded. "Oh, okay, Huckleberry."

"Not sure who this Huckleberry fella is, but I can tell by the obnoxious tone of your voice that I should be offended. Seeing as you're upset, I'm gonna let that slide," Teddy said. "For your information, my pa hid a secret stash of gold for safekeeping. If we find it, we can save the day."

"And exactly how are we gonna find this long-lost gold?"

"By putting our heads together and searching for clues.

And while we're at it, let's take down Aubrey in the school election." Teddy thrust out his hand to shake on the deal. "Partners?"

Ollie rubbed the back of his neck. *A partnership. With a ghost?* Things could be a lot worse. At least he had a new friend—even if he was dead. "Okay. Partners." He broke into a smile. "Although I have a feeling I'm gonna regret this."

Teddy punched the air in triumph. "Yes! Partners!"

Without thinking, Ollie reached out to shake his new partner's hand, but came up empty. An icy blast of cold air shot through his body, sending chills up his spine.

CHAPTER 8
NEW LETTER

Later that afternoon, Ollie stretched out on his back under the lemon tree in his front yard. A lemon landed with a soft *thud* on the lawn, inches from his forehead. His eyes snapped open. Directly above him, Teddy was perched on a branch with his back against the trunk and one foot dangling.

"That was a bit too close for comfort," Ollie grumbled.

Teddy looked down his nose at him and grinned. "Just trying to get your attention."

"A simple 'excuse me' would work."

"Fine." Teddy hopped down and landed next to Ollie. "Excuuuse me!"

"Dude!" Ollie sat up and plucked a twig from his hair. "So annoying."

"What's that, young man?" A little old lady walking her poodle stopped at the front gate. The dog growled and poked its nose through the slats of the picket fence. Baring its teeth, the little ball of fur began to bark and spin in circles. "Were you talking to me?" she asked.

"Uh . . . No." Ollie sprang to his feet and strode over to the gate. "Nice doggy," he cooed. "What's his name?"

"This is Mr. Bone Jangles," she replied with an adoring expression. "He just loves his afternoon walks." The dog scratched at the gate and barked furiously. "Oh my, he's usually so friendly. I wonder what's got him in a tizzy?"

Teddy peered over the fence. "He's a yappy little mutt, isn't he?"

"Maybe he doesn't like you," Ollie remarked.

The woman gasped. "That is a very rude thing to say, young man. My BoBo loves me. Don't you, sweetums?"

"No, wait, I . . ." Ollie stammered. "I-I wasn't talking to you. I uh—"

Teddy fell to the ground and rolled around in the grass, clutching his sides and laughing.

"Such sass," she grumbled, ambling away. "I blame those darn video games you kids play."

"Thanks a lot!" Ollie glared at Teddy. "I look like a complete jerk."

"Just a little," Teddy agreed, with a good-natured laugh. "Not my fault you can't keep your pie hole shut."

"Whatever." Ollie sat down and pulled his knees up under his chin. He wondered if Teddy had learned anything new since their last conversation. "Is Captain Cook really going to lose his building?"

"Sad, but true." Teddy pushed himself up and sat cross-legged with his back against the tree. "I paid Captain Cook a visit and while I was there, I overheard a phone conversation about an overdue loan payment."

"Yeah, yeah . . . My mom told me he was having money problems. That's why we're here. She's gonna help turn things around at the Bing."

"It may be too late." Teddy furrowed his brow. "The bank just served him a forty-five day notice to pay up. Captain Cook was pretty upset because he thought he had more time. If he misses the next payment, it's lights out at the Bing. Literally."

Ollie tugged at his eyebrow. A wave of anxiety washed over his body. The idea of moving again filled him with dread. He surveyed his house with fresh eyes. Maybe pink wasn't so bad after all. "Tell me about this gold."

"There's a hitch." Teddy scratched his chin. "The details are a bit fuzzy. My pa was worried about bandits, so he hid the gold for safekeeping. I just don't remember where."

"Do you think he hid it behind a wall in your house?" Ollie asked. "Or a secret room?"

"Possibly."

"Okay . . . you're not giving me very much to go on." Ollie scrunched up his face and concentrated. "Let's start from the beginning. Where's your house?"

"Dunno."

"Are you telling me you don't know where you lived?" Ollie screeched.

"I'm dead." Teddy inched forward and stared at him as if to say—duh. "What am I supposed to do with a house? *Live* there?"

"I can't believe you don't know where you lived. That's kinda weird, even by your standards."

"So much has changed over the years," Teddy replied in a quiet voice. "Nothing looks the same." He rubbed the side of his head like it hurt. "Some things I can remember clear as day, like my favorite food was corn on the cob. But other details, like important details, seem so fuzzy. It's like I got the sense knocked out of me. It's all very confusing."

"It's okay." Ollie could see his friend was getting upset. "What's your last name? Maybe we can get Miss Sally to look up city records or something."

"Mmmm . . . don't know."

"Let me get this straight," Ollie said, trying to keep his voice level. "You don't know where the gold is hidden, you don't know where you lived, and you don't even know your last name." He threw his hands up in the air in defeat. "Awesome!"

"When you put it that way, it doesn't feel very awesome." Teddy slumped back against the tree.

The sound of a second story window opening caused both boys to glance up.

Mom leaned over the sill and yelled down at Ollie. "Ten-minute warning!"

"I'm ready," he hollered back. "Tell señorita Sloth to get a move on. She's the one who always makes us late."

"Ten-minute warning?" Teddy asked. "What's that?"

"My sister has an open house where she takes acting classes." Ollie rolled his eyes. "As if one drama queen isn't bad enough, tonight I'll be surrounded at the Scott Street Studio of Artsy-Fartsy."

"I wanna go!" Teddy exclaimed. "I've never been to an open house. By the way, what's an open house?"

"It's a whole lotta boring, is what it is," Ollie groaned. "But we can use the time to strategize while my mom meets with DeeDee's new drama coach."

———

Twenty minutes later, Mom pulled to a stop in front of the Scott Street Studio of Performing Arts. The stately home-turned-studio sat atop a small hill behind a tall, ornate iron fence with comedy and tragedy mask cutouts fixed to the gate. At the foot of the magnificent stone steps leading to the grand entrance, twin corkscrew-shaped trees reached up to the sky. Perfectly manicured hedges surrounded the grounds, and a lone palm tree stood like a sentinel on guard. A stream of families made their way up to the studio.

"Cool," Ollie exclaimed. "It looks like the Haunted Mansion at Disneyland."

"It kind of does," Mom agreed. "Minus the ghosts, of course."

DeeDee lowered the sun visor and checked herself out in the tiny mirror. "The lighting is horrible this time of day."

"I agree." Ollie nodded. "You look way better in the dark."

"MOM!" DeeDee wailed.

"Oliver Elias Oxley!" Mom glared at him in the rear-view mirror. "Apologize. Now."

"Sorry, DoDo," he said in a not-so-sorry voice.

"That wasn't an apology." DeeDee twisted in her seat and glared at Ollie.

"Uh-huh."

"Nuh-uh."

"Uh-huh."

"Nuh-uh."

"ENOUGH!" Mom shot Ollie a death look, then whirled around and eyed DeeDee. "Are you about ready?"

Teddy chuckled. "You two really have a way with words."

"Shut it," Ollie hissed under his breath.

DeeDee dramatically inhaled and exhaled five times before finally declaring herself ready to go.

Mom met Ollie's gaze in the rearview mirror. "Don't wander off. We shouldn't be too long. I don't want to have to search for you when we're done. Remember last time?"

"I know this place." Teddy gazed out the window.

"Oh, yeah?" Ollie opened the car door and stepped onto the sidewalk. "It's about time you remembered something."

"What's that?" Mom stopped dead in her tracks.

"No-no, sorry, Mom," Ollie sputtered. "I won't wander off. Promise."

"Oh, boy." Teddy threw his head back and laughed so hard he snorted. "Somebody's in trouble."

Ollie waited until Mom and DeeDee walked out of earshot before reprimanding Teddy. "Can it, dude. So not funny."

"It's kind of funny," Teddy murmured. "You're like a walking sideshow. I haven't had this much fun in years."

"Whatever." Ollie started up the front walk. "What do you know about this place, anyway?"

"Back in my day, this wasn't a studio. It was the Briggs Mansion, home to the richest folk in all of Granite City. As a matter of fact . . ." Teddy's voice trailed off. "I just remembered something. Follow me." He darted up the front walk and vanished into the house.

"Wait!" Ollie weaved his way through the crowd and chased after him. Inside the house, he came to an abrupt halt in the entryway. *Which way did he go?*

"Over here," Teddy yelled from a doorway, waving his arms to get his attention.

Ollie hurried over and whispered, "What is it?"

"There's a secret passageway in the kitchen," Teddy said with a new sense of urgency.

"How do you know?" Ollie slipped into the kitchen. A row of pink boxes crammed full of doughnuts sat on the counter next to a large coffee canister and a stack of Styrofoam cups.

"I've been in it," Teddy replied. "I think there's something important inside."

"Like a clue?" Ollie asked with growing excitement.

"Maybe. We won't know unless we go."

"How do we get in?" Ollie asked, his adrenaline spiking. He eyed the coffee and doughnuts. People could spill into the kitchen at any moment. Time was not on his side.

"It's under there." Teddy pointed to a staircase that ascended to the second floor. "Grab the bottom step and pull up on it like it's a storm cellar door."

"No way!" Ollie ventured across the kitchen and knelt down to inspect the stairs. There were tiny brown scuff marks on the wall near the bottom step. "You're right. That's so cool!"

"What are you waiting for?" Teddy demanded. "Pull!"

Ollie cast a furtive glance over his shoulder. All clear. His pulse quickened. Bending down on one knee, he placed his fingers under the lip of the bottom wooden stair and pulled up. Dank air blasted him in the face as the staircase creaked open to reveal a passageway.

A single light bulb with a pull string hung from the low ceiling. He yanked on the cord. A pale light filled the corridor. The passageway was narrow and roughly ten feet long. A faint light seeped in through a crack in the door at the opposite end of the passageway. Exposed beams and old wood siding reminded him of a mine shaft.

"I told you." Teddy strutted by with an air of importance. "Come on."

Ollie crept forward and eased the door shut behind him. The air was chilly. Cobwebs brushed past his face. A small rodent scurried across the floor. "I hope that's not what I think it is," he sputtered, wiping away the cobwebs.

"Don't be such a pantywaist. It's just a rat."

"It's sooo easy to be brave when you're a ghost." Ollie wandered down the passageway, peering from left to right and up and down. "Where's this clue?"

Heavy footsteps overhead caused dust to rain down on Ollie's head. The sound of muffled voices through the wall created a ghostly murmur that echoed in the narrow passageway. A loud crack sounded, then everything went black.

Ollie tripped on the uneven brick floor, jamming his toe. "Ouch! Teddy, wait up." He punched the power button on his cell phone and held it up to illuminate the way. A swath of light cut through the dark.

Teddy had come to a complete standstill. He ran his fingers through his hair and down the side of his face, studying a spot on the wall. "Now, I remember," he said with a dreamy look on his face.

Ollie hurried to his partner's side and leaned in for a better look. "Is it a clue?"

Teddy passed his hand over a heart carved into a wood beam with the initials *TK + BB* still visible in its center. His eyes lit up, and a smile spread across his face. "I was sweet on Beatrice Briggs. Prettiest gal in town."

"That's your clue?" Ollie shrieked. "Your girlfriend?"

"I said *maybe* it was a clue," Teddy replied, sheepishly.

"Wait a minute." Ollie shined the light on the wall and examined the engraving. "It *is* a clue," he said, tracing the letters with his finger. "Your initials are *T. K.*"

"Yeah. So?"

"*T* is for Teddy." Ollie arched an eyebrow. "What does the *K* stand for?"

"My last name, of course!" Teddy exclaimed. "But I still can't remember what it is."

"That's okay." Ollie grinned. "Thanks to this new letter, we've got our first clue."

CHAPTER 9

NEW SHERIFF

Ollie paced back and forth in front of the school office. "I can do this." He reached for the handle, then pulled back as if shocked by static electricity.

"Are we really doing this again?" Teddy stood slanted against the door. "This is the third day in a row, and it's always the same thing: 'Should I, or shouldn't I?'" Teddy mocked in a whiny voice. "Man up! Today's the last day to sign up. It's now or never."

"Fine. I'm going in." Ollie gave a snort of surrender. "You happy now?"

"I am." Teddy grinned. "Don't be such a worry wart. What's the worst thing that could happen?"

"Hmm. I don't know . . . Social annihilation? Didn't you hear what Gurdeep said? Aubrey's gonna make my life miserable." Ollie yanked the door open, stayed unfazed as it passed through Teddy, and went inside. "Whatever."

The office looked like every other office Ollie had visited. And there had been many. To his right, four metal chairs with cracked vinyl seats sat empty. Fluorescent lights buzzed overhead. An ancient computer sat atop a large desk next to a door with the name PRINCIPAL RITTER etched into the glass of its rectangle window. The air reeked of burnt microwave popcorn and stale coffee. Other than the low murmur of voices coming from the principal's office, the room was empty.

"Where do I sign up?" Ollie wondered.

"Duh . . . Right here." Teddy gestured to a large poster on the wall. "Under the gigantic sign that says STUDENT COUNCIL ELECTION SIGN UP."

"Thanks a lot. Now, beat it. You're bugging me." Ollie picked up a pen to write his name. All five of the student council positions had at least four candidates signatures, with the exception of one. He hesitated when he saw Aubrey's name—and only Aubrey's name—listed as a candidate for seventh grade class president. *Yikes!* Before he could chicken out, he signed his name. *Take that!* Satisfied, he hurried off to class.

———

A short time later, Mr. Miller moved at a snail's pace toward his desk while reading a handout. His eyes widened in surprise and a smile tugged at the corner of his mouth. "Good morning. I have the official list of candidates for this year's student council."

Uh-oh. Ollie got a sinking feeling in the pit of his stomach. *Things are about to get ugly.*

"For the job of class president, we have two candidates: Aubrey Kelly and Ollie Oxley. For Vice—"

Aubrey gasped. Excitement rippled through the classroom. Cell phones buzzed to life. Chirps, whooshes, and dings reverberated in Ollie's ears like a series of small explosions. Slouching down in his chair, Ollie could almost feel Aubrey giving him the stink-eye.

"Phones off!" Mr. Miller demanded. "This isn't exactly *The Hunger Games*, people. Settle down." He inflated his cheeks and exhaled. "As I was saying before I was so rudely interrupted, next Friday, all the candidates will have the opportunity to earn your votes. This year, instead of speeches, candidates will set up campaign stations in the quad for you to visit. For the job of vice president, we have four candidates ..."

"Way to go," Gurdeep whispered. "You have my vote."

"Gee, thanks." Ollie shifted in his seat. His stomach pitched, as if he were bobbing on a ship in the ocean.

"I've also got a note from Aubrey." Gurdeep tossed a crumpled-up ball of paper onto his desk. "I think she's a little pissed off."

"Ya think?" Ollie's fingers tingled. Cracking his knuckles, he unfolded the wad of paper, and read the message.

YOU'RE A DEAD MAN!

Teddy peered over his shoulder and read it. "Now, that's not a nice note."

Ollie scribbled in his notebook:

I'M AFRAID TO LOOK. WHAT'S SHE DOING?

Teddy grimaced. "Let's just say, if looks could kill, we'd be spending a lot more time together."

Ollie drew an angry face and wrote:

THIS IS YOUR FAULT! WHAT'S THE PLAN?

"The plan is not to turn on your partner at the first sign of trouble. Did ya think she was gonna hand you a cookie and wish you well?"

Ollie drew a pair of horns and a goatee on the angry face and wrote:

BITE ME! WHAT'S THE PLAN?!

Teddy gazed long and hard at the note from Aubrey. "I think it's time we send a message of our own."

WHAT KIND OF MESSAGE?

"The kind that says there's a new sheriff in town."

AWESOME. YOU DO THAT WHILE I PLAY DODGE-BULLY.

Ollie slammed the notebook shut and laid his head down on his desk, wishing he could make like a ghost and disappear.

———

At lunchtime, students streamed out to the quad, heads down, shoulders hunched, texting. Ollie weaved through the crowd. *Where the heck is Teddy?* The smell of Tater Tots and pizza saturated the air, making his stomach churn. Kids whispered and nudged each other, stealing glances his way.

OLLIE OXLEY AND THE GHOST

"Look at you!" Teddy exclaimed. "You're the talk of the town."

"Mm-hmm," Ollie murmured through tight lips. He adjusted his backpack and shifted his gaze across the quad. Aubrey and the gargoyles huddled together under the oak tree, stuffing their faces with pizza. Aubrey paused mid-bite and stared straight at him, her face twisted in anger.

He gulped. Running for class president suddenly felt like a very bad idea.

"Where ya going?" Teddy trailed after him like an eager puppy. "Don't ya want to mingle with your peeps? Shake some hands? Earn some votes?"

"No." Ollie waited for a pack of girls to pass, then resumed when they'd were out of earshot. "Did you remember your last name?" he asked, feeling more than a bit grumpy. He needed to focus on something other than his impending social doom.

"No. But I'll keep trying."

"Awesome." Ollie kicked a rock. It bounced across the grass and landed at the edge of the blacktop.

"I'm beginning to think you don't know what the word *awesome* means," Teddy mumbled.

"Yeah, well, I'm beginning to think you talked me into a big, fat mess," Ollie shot back. "Aubrey's totally pissed off." He cast an uneasy glance over his shoulder. "Speaking of the nut job, now's a good time for you to make like 007 and spy. I'm gonna shoot some hoops."

"Aye, aye, captain." Teddy gave a quick salute and disappeared.

Ollie grabbed a basketball from the storage locker and headed to the blacktop. He dribbled the ball toward the basket, made a layup and missed, rebounded and shot again. From across the court, he observed a boy from science class approaching. Was he a friend or foe? Ollie's eyes traveled the boy up and down. With a bright smile and a casual swagger, the boy didn't look menacing. He had olive skin and a purple Mohawk that added at least six inches to his small stature. Dressed in board shorts and a green hoodie, he looked like a surf rat on his way to a punk rock concert.

"Hey, bro." The boy flashed a toothy grin. "Name's Cole Caccavo. Just wanted to let ya know I've got your back."

"Really?" Ollie continued to dribble the ball. "Good to know."

"Matter of fact, I've got Aubrey's back, too. See for yourself." He waggled his eyebrows in a comical fashion and tilted his Mohawk to one side.

Ollie tracked the Mohawk to Aubrey and the gargoyles. The trio circled a cluster of unsuspecting girls like vultures, dark and menacing. With an evil smirk, Aubrey swooped in and flicked a pretty brunette's phone out of her hand. "Heads up, Abby."

The phone rocketed skyward and tumbled back down to earth with a loud *crack*.

"Hey!" Abby scrambled to retrieve her phone. "If it's broken—"

"If it's broken what?" Aubrey taunted, holding out her hands, palms up. "What exactly are you gonna do about it?"

Abby retrieved the phone and turned it over a couple of times, inspecting it for cracks. "Get a life."

"I've already got one, loser." Aubrey made an about face and strutted away, high-fiving the gargoyles. A smattering of snickers followed her like the beginning of a rainfall, slow and steady, eventually erupting into a full swell of laughter.

Abby held up her phone and snapped a picture of Aubrey. "Nice sign. Who's the loser now?"

"I don't get it," Ollie said. "What's so funny?"

"Wait for it . . ." Cole dragged out the sentence like a magician revealing his trick.

Aubrey stopped and slowly rotated in a complete circle. "Why's everyone laughing?" she demanded.

"Now!" Cole shouted. "Look!"

At first, Ollie didn't see anything unusual or funny. Then a sudden breeze kicked up a sign taped to Aubrey's back. The paper fluttered in the wind, letting him catch sight of the words *Vote Ollie Oxley for Class President* written in bold red lettering.

Oh, boy! This is not going to end well.

"What a moron!" Cole howled, doubling over with laughter. "That's going viral."

"Don't look now," warned Ollie. "But that moron is headed our way."

Aubrey pushed past Cinda and Sierra and stomped across the blacktop. "What are you laughing at, Coleslaw?" she snarled, jabbing a finger at Cole's chest.

"Why don't you ask your zombies?" Cole flipped up his hoodie and lumbered toward the gargoyles, arms sticking straight out. "Grrrrrrrrrr."

Aubrey glowered at the Cinda and Sierra. "What's he talking about?"

"He—he—he might be talking about the sign on your back," Sierra stammered.

"Sign?" Aubrey shrieked with a crazed expression. "What sign?"

Cinda picked her nose as if the answer might pop out in the form of a booger.

Sierra ripped the sign off of Aubrey's shirt and handed it to her, shrinking back in alarm.

Aubrey gawked at the paper in her hands. "What the—" She paused to wipe a fleck of spittle from her lips. "Why didn't you idiots say something?"

"W—w—we thought maybe you put it there," Sierra sputtered.

"Why would I do that?" Aubrey's face blazed fire-engine

red. "*I'm* running for class president!" The bell sounded. She shoved the paper into Cole's chest and stomped off, leaving Cinda and Sierra rooted to the spot.

"Saved by the bell." Cole slapped the sign onto Cinda's back. "You two morons may want to watch your backs."

"Stuff it, Coleslaw," Cinda growled, pushing him away.

"I'd rather be a tasty salad than a creeper like you. It looks like your world is about to blow!" Cole hissed, then he made explosion sounds and crumpled to the ground.

"Come on." Sierra grabbed Cinda by the arm and pulled her away. "Later, losers." The two girls marched back to class. The sign on Cinda's back tilted to one side, but the message was clear.

"Nice exploding creeper." Ollie reached out and gave Cole a hand up. "By the way, how come you're not afraid of Aubrey?"

"Let's just say I've got a little dirt on her. We go way back. In preschool, her nickname was Smelly Kelly."

"Smelly Kelly?" Ollie tossed the basketball into the storage locker. "How'd she get that?"

"She had a bad habit of pooping her pants whenever she got mad." Cole plugged his nose. "Which was like, every day."

"Ew!" Ollie made a *yuck* face. "But how does that help you now?"

"It's hard to be taken seriously as the Queen of Mean when you have a nickname like Smelly Kelly."

"Smelly Kelly." Teddy rubbed his hands together. "I think I can put that to good use."

Ollie gave a choked cry as if a giant bug had flown up his nose.

Cole gave him a curious sidelong glance. "Bro? You okay?"

"Fine." Ollie glowered at Teddy. "Just an annoying pest."

"Tsk, tsk," Teddy chided. "I have an idea. See you in a few."

"See ya." Ollie knelt down to tie his shoelaces. Students surged past him on their way to class.

"Bro, I'm in your class," Cole said. "I sit right behind you."

"Oh, right." Ollie shook his head. "I didn't want to make you late for class," he added to cover his tracks. "Cruz can be a nightmare if you're late." He finished tying the laces on his right shoe and stood up. "Let's go."

The two boys lined up with their classmates outside room twenty-two. Miss Cruz flipped through a set of keys. After fumbling with the lock, she opened the door. One by one, the students filed through the doorway and into the class-room. Ollie moseyed over to his desk, scouring the room for any sign of Teddy. His eyes finally came to rest on scratchy handwriting scrawled across the whiteboard.

AUBREY ~~KELLY~~ SM STINKS FOR CLASS PRESIDENT!

"Oi!" Aubrey's head snapped around to face Ollie. "You bloody well did this, Oxley."

"I was at lunch," Ollie said with a bland face. "Same as you." He slid into his seat and dropped his backpack on the desk with a loud *thud*.

The message sent everyone into fits of laughter. However, Miss Cruz was not amused. Drawing her lips into a tight line, she turned her back on the class. When she was done cleaning the whiteboard, she turned back around and spoke, "I'm not sure who did this, but it's not funny." Her piercing gaze moved slowly from student to student. "I will not tolerate bullying in my class." The room stirred with jittery hands and feet, but no one made a peep. "Is that understood?"

Ollie's breath caught in his throat. *Bullying?* He slid down in his chair and dropped his chin to his chest.

"If no one has anything to say, let's get to work." Miss Cruz opened her textbook. "Today we are conducting an experiment with warm and cold expanding air. This will require a balloon, hot water, cold water, and . . ."

Cole tapped Ollie on the shoulder. "Bro, I have a note."

"As much as I love Aubrey's notes, I'll pass," Ollie whispered under his breath.

"It's not from you-know-who." Cole slipped the note onto Ollie's desk. "It's from Mikayla Mims."

What could she possibly want with me? Ollie cast a look over his right shoulder.

Up until now, he'd never made eye contact with Mikayla. For good reason. She was the prettiest girl in school. He feared his brain would turn to mush. He gulped. The slender girl twirled a pencil between her brown fingers and arched a delicate eyebrow at him. "Read my note," she mouthed.

Ollie's heart beat faster, and his throat felt dry. He glanced down at his mismatched socks. Embarrassed, he tucked his feet under his chair. Palming the note, he turned it over in his hands then held it up to his nose. It smelled like strawberries. He carefully unfolded the pink paper and read the message: I VOTE OLLIE OXLEY FOR CLASS PRESIDENT.

"Now, that is a nice note," said Teddy. "I guess she got the message that there's a new sheriff in town."

CHAPTER 10
NEW SLOGAN

VOTE FOR OLLIE, BY GOLLY. "Blech! I need a new slogan." Ollie collapsed onto his bed and scratched through the last line in his notebook. He turned to a fresh page, and he immediately drew a blank. Staring off into space, he flipped the pencil back and forth between two fingers.

A cold draft stirred the balls of paper strewn about the floor. Gus growled, drew back his ears, and belly-crawled across the room to the red beanbag chair. A line of fur rose along his spine. Then, as if poked by an invisible finger, he yelped and sprang vertically into the air like a four-legged pogo stick.

"Greetings and salutations from the other side!" hailed Teddy. "I bring news from the enemy camp."

"Jeez!" Ollie startled. "I almost wet my pants! Not to mention poor Gus is gonna need doggy therapy. Seriously. Rattle some chains or something."

"Boooring. You think because I'm a ghost I should rattle chains? Peach-bombs? Yes. Tripping snot-faced bullies. Definitely. But chains? Never."

Ollie's mouth fell open. "That was you?"

Teddy puffed out his chest and hooked his thumbs on his suspenders. "You think that's good? I used to help Miss Sally when she hosted séances by shaking a table or knocking on a wall to give her street cred."

"Street cred? What are you, a ghost rapper? No. Never mind." Ollie covered his ears with his hands. "Wait a minute . . ." He lowered his hands and narrowed his eyes. "Are you Miss Sally's imaginary friend?"

"Guilty as charged." Teddy held up his right hand. "She used to be my best friend."

"What happened? Did you guys have a fight or something?"

"Nooo!" Teddy shook his head. "Having me around ruined her life. So I went away and stayed away. It seemed like the right thing to do."

"The right thing to do? You dropped out of her life and made her a social outcast." Ollie envisioned a future with a nickname like *Oddball Ollie*. Was he doomed to a similar fate? "Is Miss Sally really a medium?"

"It depends on your definition of *medium*. If you mean, as a rule, can she communicate with the dead? Then, no. If you mean did she have a friend who was dead? Then, yes," Teddy added, flashing a mischievous smile.

"Let me get this straight; after you vanished for good, you led her to believe that she could talk to *other* ghosts?"

Ollie gave Teddy the stink-eye. "Not cool, dude. I think you owe her an apology."

"Speaking of apologies . . ." Teddy's voice trailed off. "I may owe you a teensy, weensy, little apology." He held his first finger and thumb about an inch apart.

Ollie squinted and lowered his chin. "What did you do now?"

"Well . . . When you first moved in, I didn't know we were gonna be friends."

"Mmm-hmm," Ollie murmured. "Go on."

"Well." Teddy grimaced and glanced away. "It wasn't DeeDee who turned on your alarm clock and maybe you *did* unpack those family photos."

"What?" Ollie exclaimed. "Why would you do that?"

"Sorry." Teddy frowned. "I was bored. And well, you were kind of a grump. I thought you could use a little shaking up."

Ollie swallowed the urge to lash out, but decided to just let it go. He had bigger fish to fry, namely one swampy bottom feeder by the name of Aubrey Kelly. "Never mind. What did you find out about the campaign?"

Teddy flopped down onto the bean bag chair. Sometimes Ollie forgot that Teddy was a ghost. He looked and acted so much like a real boy—except for the disappearing acts, of course.

"Here's the deal," Teddy began. "During assembly, Little Miss Poopy-Pants, Stinky, and Dinky plan on handing out balloons that say *UP, UP AND AWAY WITH AUBREY*. Stupid, if you ask me, unless it literally means up, up and away with Aubrey. Then, it's stupendous!" Teddy chuckled.

"Speaking of the whole poopy-pants thing," Ollie said speaking in slow, halting words. "Maybe we should go easy on the name calling. I wanna beat Aubrey at her own game, but I don't wanna be like her. Know what I mean?"

"So you want me to be nice to her?" Teddy asked, his face a ball of confusion.

"No!" Ollie laughed. "She's still a butthead. I just don't want to sink to her level."

"Got it." Teddy gave a thumbs up. "No more Poopy-Pants. Speaking of Poopy-Pants, err, I mean Aubrey, when she's at home she drifts in and out of her British accent. One minute she's talking like a deranged Hermione Granger, next thing ya know, she slips up and talks like a normal Granite City kid."

"How do you know about Hermione Granger?"

"I may be dead, but I still love a good movie." Teddy snorted with indignation. "There are fringe benefits to being a ghost. I get to see all the best movies, free of charge. Occasionally, I'll even sneak into an R-rated movie."

"Yeah, well, considering you're like over a hundred and fifty years old—and dead—I doubt anyone's gonna care."

It suddenly dawned on Ollie that he'd never bothered to ask Teddy how he passed the time. For that matter, he'd never bothered to ask how he passed away. Was it proper to ask such a thing? *I bet even Google doesn't have the answer to that.* He cleared his throat. "So, like, um, if you don't mind me asking, how exactly did you die?"

For a nanosecond, Teddy flickered like a light bulb the moment before it burns out. A haunted expression crossed over his face. "I fell and hit my noggin." He winced at the painful memory of his demise. "And then everything went black."

A grim silence hung in the air.

"Do you miss your family?" Ollie asked, feeling twitchy and uncomfortable.

"Every day," Teddy answered. "I really miss my little brother, Eli. He told the best jokes," he added, his blue eyes lost in the past. "Let's see if I can remember one." A smile inched its way across his face. "Oh. Oh. Oh. What do you get from a pampered cow?"

Ollie favored him with a blank stare. "Dunno."

"Spoiled milk." Teddy guffawed and slapped his leg. "What a madcap!"

"Weird," Ollie observed. "You can remember a bad joke, but you can't remember your last name or where you lived."

"My memory is funny that way." Teddy rubbed the side of his head. "Anyway, back to the election. How do you plan on taking Aubrey down?"

"I've got an idea." Ollie tapped his chin, the beginning of a plan formulating. "But we need Captain Cook's help."

"Jumpin' catfish! Are we going to throw rock candy at Aubrey?"

"Tempting. But no. We need a special batch of candy that'll blow away the competition." Ollie leaned back against the headboard and stretched his arms out behind his head. "Tomorrow, we go to Cook's."

"Sounds like a plan," Teddy agreed. "Next order of business: the gold."

"I've been thinking about that." Ollie sat up, swung his legs off the bed, and crossed the room to a pile of dirty clothes. Crouching, he dug through his smelly laundry until he found the pair of shorts he wanted. Reaching into the back pocket, he pulled out a folded piece of paper. "I got this from Miss Sally," he said, showing Teddy the brochure. "It's all about Granite City history."

Teddy examined the mustard-colored trifold with carefully printed black text and old photographs. Ollie plunked down on the pile of clothes, unfolded the brochure, and smoothed it out on his knee. He briefly skimmed the narrow columns then read it out loud, "In 1848, the California Gold Rush began when gold was discovered at Sutter's Mill in Coloma, California, by James W. Marshall. In 1849 treasure hunters—called forty-niners—converged on Granite City. Forty-niners panned for gold in the riverbeds and streams."

He stopped reading and stared meaningfully at Teddy. "I think your dad was a forty-niner."

"My pa did spend many a long day down at the river, panning for gold."

"If your dad had so much gold he had to hide it, I bet he was someone important. Maybe there's a record of somebody with a last name that starts with a *K*. Let's ask Miss Sally for help. It's time you man up and apologize for skipping out on her and making her think she's something she's not."

"I'll take it into consideration," Teddy grumbled. "You don't know Miss Sally, she can hold a grudge like nobody's business."

"Deal with it!" Ollie threw a dirty sock at Teddy—it whizzed through him and knocked over a can of soda. "We need her help."

"All right, already. But for now, how about a friendly game of hangman?" Teddy suggested. "Eli and I used to play every night."

Hours later, after losing six games of hangman, Ollie slammed his pencil on the floor and yelled, "Cheater! That's it. I'm done." He ripped the paper out of the notebook and tossed it into the trash. "You're making up words."

"Goodle?" Teddy snorted. "I can't believe you fell for 'goodle' as a word."

"I fell for it because you told me it meant panning for gold with your toes. Why wouldn't I believe it? Look at your feet!" Ollie shrieked. "Whatever! I'm going to bed." With that said, he turned off the light, pulled up the covers and rolled over to go to sleep. "Leave!"

"Goodle night and sweet dreams." Teddy giggled and disappeared into the night.

CHAPTER 11

NEW EMAIL

Teddy stood at Miss Sally's front door. He tapped his fingers against his leg. A nagging doubt pushed its way to the forefront of his mind. *Is Ollie right? Did I do wrong by Miss Sally?* Riddled with guilt, he decided it was time to pay her a visit. Before he could change his mind, he took a tentative step through the front door and into the living room.

The light from a frilly floor lamp filled the room with a pleasant glow. A green hand-knotted rug covered the hardwood floor. Shelves full of books covered one wall, floral prints adorned another. A comfy lavender sofa and loveseat formed a cozy seating area in front of the brick fireplace. The sound of classical music played softly from a CD player atop an end table.

Miss Sally sat on the floor with her legs tucked under her, sorting through stacks of old black and white photographs. With great care, she scrutinized one picture through a magnifying glass. "Hello, Teddy."

Can she see me? I haven't materialized. Teddy zipped around the room, searching for a place to hide. Peeking out from behind the loveseat, he observed Miss Sally dabbing her eyes as she gazed at the photograph and said, "I've missed you."

He crept over to get a better view of the picture. *Jumpin' catfish! That's my family.* His Ma and Pa stood arm in arm on the front porch of the family home. He and Eli sat on the stoop, dressed in their Sunday best. It was a tight shot, so not much of the house was visible, but even so, memories came flooding back through time. It was the very day his Pa struck gold—hit the mother lode. They were rich. Very rich. A photographer from the *Granite City Gazette* had come out to take their picture. Later that same day, Pa buried the gold for safekeeping, fearful bandits might try and steal their windfall.

As if sensing someone, Miss Sally lowered the photograph and cast her gaze around the room. Teddy did not move. Ollie was right, he needed to make amends, but now was not the right time. This apology required a well-thought-out plan—one that involved serious groveling. He glided through the kitchen wall and into the night.

A full moon shone bright overhead. Teddy strolled down the quiet street whistling a jaunty tune. *Ollie is going to be so happy when I tell him I finally remembered something.*

A white cat jumped out from behind a hedge and darted across the street. Teddy slowed his pace as he got closer to Aubrey's house. He shuddered at the thought of who he might bump into upon his arrival.

In the 1800s, the Kelly residence had served as the town courthouse—and gallows. The trials of murderers and thieves took place on the main floor. If found guilty, the convicted were taken to the basement and hanged. Justice came so swiftly, it left some of the condemned to wonder, "What the heck just happened?" Thus, a ragtag gaggle of misfit ghosts set up camp and refused to leave.

Teddy ducked behind a parked car when he spotted three ghosts lurking in the shadows. *Oh, no*, he cursed. *The Bickering Bandits*. The Bixby Boys, aka the Bickering Bandits of 1855, were notorious, not for their heists, but their downfall. After successfully robbing the Granite City Bank, the three brothers proceeded to quarrel over who got to carry the loot. The squabbling turned into fisticuffs that quickly spilled onto the street. The local sheriff happened upon the scene and promptly made an arrest. Three days later the brothers were tried, convicted, and hanged.

From his hiding spot, Teddy caught sight of a man out for a walk with his dog. *Crackers and crawfish. Here they go*. He settled back down to wait and watch the numskulls in action.

"Hot dang! Here comes Old Man Wigglesworth," yelled One-Eyed Walden.

"You take the mutt. Wigglesworth is mine," hollered Slippery Sam.

"No, sirree. It's my turn. You couldn't scare a fly," Bucktooth Tom shouted, pushing Slippery Sam out of the way.

Teddy watched the three bickering bozos argue back and forth, like toddlers fighting over a toy train. Meanwhile, Wigglesworth wandered by, oblivious to the spirited debate taking place.

Teddy jumped out from behind the car and strolled through the front gate. "Good job, boys. You really scared the pants off him."

"Hey," One-Eyed Walden cried. "This is our house. No new ghouls. Them's the rules."

Teddy gave a slight bow of his head in greeting. "Just visiting, gents."

"Ya best be, sonny boy," warned Bucktooth Tom. "We don't want any newbies. We've already got a full house."

"Last thing we need is a young whipper-snapper like you," Slippery Sam added, wagging his finger in the air.

"Yes, sir," Teddy acknowledged, inclining his head. "I'll be gone before you know it."

The lime-green house was run-down and gloomy, the drab curtains drawn tight. A trio of garden gnomes greeted Teddy with stony stares, their paint chipped and peeled. He poked his head through the front door. Mismatched furniture crowded the house in muted shades of dull. The dim glow from an overhead light offered little cheer.

Mrs. Kelly sat on the couch chomping on a bowl of pork

rinds. A show about misbehaving housewives blared on the television. *Business as usual.* The Kellys maintained a steady diet of reality TV and junk food. He stepped through the door and into the living room.

Aubrey sat on the floor with a laptop by her feet and a cell phone in her hand. A half-eaten box of Cook's candy lay by her side. Her fingers flew across the phone screen, texting at a breakneck pace. *What's got her bee a buzzing?* Teddy plopped down on the floor next to her and read the text:

TO: CINDA, SIERRA: *I will crush Oxley.*

"That's what you think." Teddy chuckled as he swiped delete.

"Aubrey, get me a can of soda," Mrs. Kelly demanded. Her gaping mouth revealed a chunk of pork rind wedged between her two front teeth.

"What the . . .?" Aubrey scrolled up and down her messages.

"Now! As in today," Mrs. Kelly huffed. "Are you deaf or just lazy?"

"I'm going." Aubrey scrambled to her feet and hustled to the kitchen. She opened the refrigerator door and took stock of its contents. After pushing aside a Pietro's Pizza box and a bucket of Fanny's Fried Chicken, she found a Cherry Coke hiding behind a jar of pickled pig's feet. She blew crumbs off the top of the can, then hurried back and handed the drink to her mom.

Without so much as a thank you, Mrs. Kelly cracked open the soda, chugged it down, wiped her mouth, and belched like a toad. "Have you got that campaign locked up?" she asked, between licks of her greasy fingers. "I expect you to win. I'm not raising a loser."

Aubrey's shoulders sagged and her face went slack. "Yes, ma'am."

Mrs. Kelly harrumphed and went back to watching television.

Aubrey lowered her gaze and gnawed on her thumb. All of her fingernails were chewed down to the quick. From where Teddy sat, she suddenly looked very small, neither scary nor mean. *Poor kid.*

With nothing better to do, he decided to stick around for a while and watch TV. Maybe if he hung out long enough, he'd learn something new. Two reality shows later, he hit the jackpot.

Aubrey peered over the top of her computer. "Mom, you just got a new email."

"Let me see." Mrs. Kelly yanked the laptop out of her hands and scanned the email, reading every word with growing excitement. "Yes!"

"Good news?" Aubrey asked.

"You could say that." Mrs. Kelly pounded away at the keys. "I just bought Captain Cook's loan from the bank."

"Bought the loan?" Aubrey asked, her eyes glazed over in confusion. "I don't understand."

"It means now Cook owes me the money." Mrs. Kelly punched the SEND button and chortled. "And I'm only giving him five days to pay up. When he fails to deliver, and he will, the Bingham and Beans Building will finally be mine!"

Aubrey's face screwed up. "What about Cook's Candy?"

"Gone!"

"Gone?" Aubrey murmured, gazing down at her box of candy.

"Yes. Gone. No more Cook's Candy. No more Bing." Mrs. Kelly picked her teeth with a matchbook cover. "But don't you dare tell a soul. I wanna break the news to Cook myself."

"But I love Cook's," Aubrey said softly. "I thought you were just gonna shut down the Bing. What are you gonna do with the building?"

"I'm opening a restaurant," she said, flicking a crumb off her blouse. "Kelly's Krispy Fried Delights. We'll serve fried pickles, fried mac-n-cheese, fried ravioli, fried cupcakes, fried onions, fried ice cream, fried okra, fried zucchini . . ."

Five days! Teddy sat up in alarm. *Holy-moly! We're in deep-fried doo-doo.*

CHAPTER 12
NEW BALLOONS

The big day had finally arrived—Student Council Assembly.

With slightly shaky hands, Ollie rolled up the banner he'd painted the night before and fastened it with a rubber band. Opening one of the six Cook's Candy boxes, he checked on the contents for the umpteenth time. The lollipops were two inches in diameter and covered in gold foil. A round silver label attached to the front read OLLIE-POP.

Satisfied that he was good to go, he tucked the banner under his right arm, gathered up the boxes, and wobbled out of the room. Gus jumped off the bed and followed close behind. The smell of scrambled eggs made his stomach curdle. Breathing through his mouth, he balanced the boxes on his hip, plucked his backpack off the coat rack, and reached for the front door.

"Here, sweetie, let me get that for you." Mom hurried down the hall. "Are you nervous?"

"No. I'm good." He kept his gaze trained on the threadbare rug. The swirling red and green pattern matched how his stomach felt—twisted and tied up.

"You know what I tell my actors when they get nervous?"

Mom lifted his chin to meet her eyes. "Picture everyone in their underwear. Works every time."

"Mom, this isn't some lame play," he grumbled, shifting the weight of the boxes to keep them from toppling over. He looked up at his mom. "Sorry, I didn't mean—"

"It's okay." She gave him a quick peck on the cheek and opened the door. "Good luck, sweetie."

Ollie froze momentarily, unable to move. He sucked in a deep breath of air to clear the lump in his throat. "Thanks, Mom." Squaring his shoulders, he walked out the door, pausing to wipe his feet on the red *Welcome Home* mat for good luck. *I need all the help I can get.*

Outside, the weather was warm and the sky was blue. The fresh air helped clear his mind and settled his stomach. A gentle breeze ruffled his hair and jangled the neighbor's wind chimes. He tottered down the stairs under the weight of the boxes and unloaded his campaign materials into the red wagon he'd attached to his bike using a bungee cord. "You can do this," he muttered to himself. "Aubrey's nothing more than a whack-a-doodle with a bad accent."

"People are gonna think you're a nut job if you keep talking to yourself," Teddy observed from his favorite perch in the lemon tree.

Ollie flinched. "They probably already do. No thanks to you, I might add."

"Not everyone. Just a few buttheads, but they don't count,"

Teddy reassured him. "Speaking of buttheads . . . Don't let Aubrey, Doofus, and Goofus get you down. You may feel like a loser, but we both know you're a winner."

"Gee, thanks," Ollie grumbled.

"You're welcome," Teddy replied with too much perkiness.

"Don't forget to do your part," Ollie warned. "If you blow it, I don't stand a ghost of a chance. No offense."

"None taken." Teddy hopped down and crawled into the wagon. "I think I'll hitch a ride. This way, I can keep an eye out for trouble, aka Aubrey Kelly."

"Just no more talking." Ollie tugged at his eyebrow. "Your pep talk wasn't exactly inspirational."

"But there's something important I need to tell you," Teddy said with a sense of urgency. "Last night I was—"

"Zip it." Ollie jerked his thumb and forefinger across his mouth as if closing an imaginary zipper. "Not. Another. Word."

"Fine." Teddy's face fell and he slumped down in the wagon. "But after school, we need to have a serious discussion."

"Whatever it is, it can wait." Ollie climbed onto his bike and started pedaling. "Right now, I just need to focus on the election." The wagon bounced over a pothole, jostling the candy boxes. Ollie glimpsed over his shoulder to check on his cargo. Teddy gave a thumbs-up but kept his mouth shut. *That's a first.*

Ten minutes and a few more bumps in the road later, Ollie slowed to a crawl. Students converged on the school from all directions, arriving on foot, bikes, scooters, skateboards, and unloading from cars. He pushed forward, deep in thought. *What if my plan doesn't work? What if Teddy—*

"Good luck today, bro!" Cole cheered as he cruised up on his skateboard.

Whoa! Ollie swerved to avoid crashing head-on into the crossing guard then over-corrected and came within inches of taking out a boy from homeroom. The wagon tilted precariously from side to side. "Thanks a lot, Cole," he grumbled, white-knuckling the handlebars.

"No problemo." Cole grinned and flashed a peace sign. "Don't let the haters bring you down today," he shouted over his shoulder.

"Don't worry about me. I got this." Ollie gave a feeble wave of his hand. "A little help would be nice."

"What am I?" Teddy demanded. "Chopped liver?"

Ollie opened his mouth to reply, but immediately snapped it shut when he spotted Aubrey handing out campaign flyers. Coasting to a stop, he got off his bike and looked nonchalantly over his shoulder. That's when he noticed something completely unexpected and uplifting. Tons of kids were wearing mismatched socks. He glanced down at his white sock and black sock. His heart swelled with hope. Things were looking up.

"Somebody's trolling for votes." Teddy nodded toward Aubrey, who was winding her way through the crowded parking lot. Most students shook their heads and turned away. One girl lifted her foot and pointed at her sock.

"Oi! Oxley." Aubrey broke away from a pack of kids, nudging Sierra and Cinda to follow. Sensing a confrontation, Ollie squared his shoulders and turned to face his nemesis.

"I thought for sure you'd chicken out today." Her lip twisted into a sneer and her chin jutted forward.

"That's what happens when you think." Ollie took a step closer. Her breath reeked of peanut butter. "Maybe you should give your little pea brain a rest."

"What's up with the boxes?" She purred. "Did your mummy already lose her job?"

"What are you babbling about?" Fear crept into his voice.

"That's for me to know and you to find out," she replied with a slithery smile. "Time is running out, quicker than you think. Tick-tock. Tick-tock. Tick-tock."

The gargoyles laughed dutifully.

Ollie was too stunned to say a thing.

"I got this." Teddy charged through Aubrey, who yelped as if zapped by a bolt of electricity. Her curly hair went stick-straight. Campaign flyers jumped from her hand and scattered in the wind.

"What the—" she cried, scrambling to retrieve her handouts.

Cinda and Sierra quickly joined in on the chase, leaving Ollie and Teddy by themselves.

"What do you think she meant by that?" Ollie tugged at his eyebrow. "Captain Cook still has a month to get the money."

"Ignore her." Teddy's features clouded over as he fiddled with his suspenders. "She's just trying to get your goat."

"Get my goat? What does that even mean?"

"It means she'll say anything to throw you off your game today. Go to class. I'll keep her busy."

After a small hesitation, Ollie nodded, then he remembered what Teddy had said earlier. "Hey, was there something important you wanted to tell me?"

"No," Teddy replied a bit too quickly. "It's not important. We'll talk later."

An uneasy worry washed over Ollie. What did Aubrey know? Trying his best to shake it off, he shouldered his backpack and gathered up his campaign materials. With a backward glance, he caught sight of Teddy zigzagging across the parking lot, papers rippling in his wake.

Chimes, chirps, and ringtones echoed down the corridor as students scrambled to get in the last word before the second bell. Ollie weaved through the bustling hallway until he arrived at the quad.

Rickety card tables lined the borders of the grassy area. Ollie picked an open table underneath the oak tree where he and Teddy first met. Sweeping away a smattering of leaves and acorns, he stacked the boxes on top of one another and taped the banner to the front of his table. After checking to make sure everything was secure, he sprinted to class.

The second bell rang just as he arrived at homeroom. Minutes later, Aubrey and the gargoyles turned up, sweaty and out of breath. The three girls stumbled into class, pushing and shoving each other out of the way. Mr. Miller was not amused. "Welcome to class, ladies. You've just earned yourself a detention."

"Sorry we're late," Aubrey replied, in a silky-sweet voice. "We ran into a problem." With a wicked glint in her eye, she sauntered by Ollie and swung her backpack, knocking the books off his desk. "But it's going away soon," she hissed. "Real soon."

Ollie locked eyes with her. "Whatever. I'm not the one with a detention slip," he said, gathering his tumbled books.

Mr. Miller waited for the girls to take a seat before speaking. "Today, I want to talk about the Garden Project . . ."

"Boy, she sure looks mad." Teddy chuckled. "I hope she brought snacks for detention."

Ollie shook with silent laughter.

"If you want, I'll knock her books to the floor."

A chuckle escaped Ollie's lips before he clamped a hand over his mouth.

"Hello . . . Mr. Oxley?" Mr. Miller stopped talking and

strode across the class with an angry expression on his face. He loomed large over Ollie, hands on his hips. "I don't suppose you know the answer?"

"Answer?" He gulped, his eyes flicked around the classroom. Everyone's head swiveled toward him like a mob of meerkats. *What's the question?*

Gurdeep breathed down his neck and mumbled, "Just say *organic.*"

"Yes, thank you, Gurdeep, the correct answer is *organic,*" said Mr. Miller. "And because you enjoy helping others, you are now commander in chief of the Garden Project. Translation: you're in charge of clean up."

Ollie scrunched down in his seat and whispered out the side of his mouth, "Sorry."

"As I was saying," Mr. Miller continued, "Today we break ground on the Tenth Annual Garden Project. This year's theme is the Perfect Salad. Our task is to grow all the fruits and vegetables we think make a delicious salad." He reached under his desk and pulled out a box marked Fruits and Veggies. "I would like to cast my vote for the heirloom tomato. They are perfection," he added, holding up a packet of tomato seeds. "Does anyone else have a personal favorite?"

Several hands in the class shot up. Mr. Miller's eyes roamed over the class. Aubrey waved her hand, squirming in her chair to get noticed. "Yes?" Mr. Miller acknowledged her with a curt nod. "What's your go-to at the salad bar?"

"Squash," she smirked, smooshing her thumb into the palm of her hand. "As in, squash the competition."

At this, giggles rippled through the classroom. Ollie kept his eyes trained straight ahead. *Rule number two: Never let them see you sweat.*

Mr. Miller shot Aubrey a warning look and gave a small huff of annoyance. "Let's move on . . ."

For the next hour, Mr. Miller droned on about sustainable food systems while Ollie stared intently at the clock, willing the big hand to move faster. Fifteen minutes until the bell rings. He tugged at his eyebrow. Thirteen. He opened his binder and doodled on the back of last week's math test. The "D" he'd earned required a parent's signature. With campaign on the brain, he'd totally forgotten to have it signed.

The bell rang. Ollie slammed his binder shut. The impact sent his math test sailing across the room, but he didn't notice. It landed under a desk, three rows back. He grabbed his backpack and rushed out of the classroom.

A steady flow of students surged toward the multipurpose room. Ollie wiggled through the sea of kids like a salmon swimming upstream until he arrived at his campaign table. Dropping his backpack on the ground, he reached for a box. "What the—" Furious, he brushed away dead leaves to uncover a bright red sign splashed across the top of the Cook's Candy boxes—LOSER! He whirled around and scanned the crowd.

On the opposite side of the quad, Aubrey was sitting at her station surrounded by colorful balloons. The gargoyles stood by her side with blank expressions pasted on their faces. She glared at him and then placed an L on her forehead and mouthed, "Loser."

Ollie held up a W sign using his thumbs and forefingers and mouthed, "Whatever." Turning his back on Aubrey, he ripped a box open and started arranging Ollie-Pops on the table with the sticks facing out.

"Boo!" Teddy sprang out from behind the tree.

Ollie yelped and jerked backward. The box sprang out of his hands and into the air. Ollie-Pops rained down in the shade of the oak tree. "Come on! You gotta stop popping up like a toaster strudel."

"Sorry." Teddy's blue eyes glinted mischievously.

"You make me look like a complete dork."

"No one's even looking," Teddy said in a not-so-convincing tone. "Well, except for Aubrey, Meanie, and Weenie."

Ollie snatched a peek over his shoulder. All three girls were laughing. Shaking his head, he knelt down to gather the candy. Dirt and leaves clung to the wrappers. He carefully wiped each one on his shorts.

"Never mind them. Today's gonna be a blast."

"It better be." Ollie scouted around for the last of the candy, but stopped short when he noticed a book-sized plaque nailed to the trunk of the oak tree. *What the heck?*

The dappled sunlight filtering through the branches obscured his view, so he inched forward to read the engraving:

DEDICATED TO
MARTIN K. KELLY – 1899.

FOR GENEROUSLY DONATING
THIS LAND TO GRANITE CITY.

Alarm bells went off inside his head. He gaped at the
plaque, then at Kelly Hall, then at Aubrey, then back at the
plaque. K as in Kelly. K as in Aubrey Kelly! *That's what she
meant by clout.* "Oh no!" Ollie gasped, rocking back on his
heels. *K as in Teddy Kelly?*

"What's wrong?" Teddy frowned.

"Nothing." Ollie cast his glance away. "Not important."

"Are you sure?" Teddy studied his face with a critical eye.
"Doesn't seem like nothing. You look like you've just seen a
ghost—pardon the expression."

Ollie caught another uneasy glimpse of the plaque. Was
Teddy a Kelly?

"Earth to Ollie." Teddy waved his hand in front of Ollie's
face. "We have company."

"What?" Ollie shook his head clear.

"It's go time!" Teddy exclaimed.

Kids began to trickle out from the multipurpose room. Students laughed and talked as they crisscrossed the quad to visit candidates. Aubrey chased down a couple of boys Ollie knew from gym, Carlos and Sebastian Garcia. The twins each grabbed a balloon and moved onto the next station.

"Here comes Cole and Gurdeep." Teddy tilted his head toward the library. "Oh, boy! They've got balloons."

"Don't forget to focus," Ollie said in a hushed voice. "Go!"

"Yes, sir!" Teddy tipped an imaginary hat and disappeared.

Ollie waited impatiently for kids to walk his way. *Come on. Come on.* He shifted from foot to foot. He crossed his fingers behind his back, hoping his far-fetched scheme would work. Cole and Gurdeep meandered over and read his banner.

JOIN THE OLLIE-POP SENSATION.
FOR IDEAS THAT ROCK—VOTE OLLIE FOR CLASS PRESIDENT.

"Yo!" Cole flashed a hang-ten sign. A pink balloon trailed behind him, bouncing in the wind.

"Nice balloon," Ollie smirked.

"Sorry, bro." Cole raised his eyebrows up and down twice and flashed a wide grin. "It's the Italian in me. I'm a lover, not a fighter. I snagged a balloon for a cute little redhead by the name of Brooke. Can't fight true love."

Ollie turned his attention to Gurdeep. "Don't even get me started on you."

"What was I supposed to do?" Gurdeep replied in a glum sort of way. "She shoved it into my hand."

"Dude, suck it up," Ollie said. "Stop letting her push you around."

"I know," Gurdeep replied in a pitiful whimper. "So, what flavor is it?" he asked, trying to change the subject.

"It's a Pop Rocks lollipop," Ollie said, with the emphasis on *pop*.

"Sweet." Cole snagged an Ollie-Pop.

POP!

The balloon exploded with a loud *bang*.

A large scrap of pink latex hit newcomer Carlos Garcia in the eye. "Ouch! What's up with that?"

"Hey!" Cole exclaimed. "That was for Brooke."

"You got pink eye," joked Carlos's twin brother, Sebastian.

Gurdeep grabbed an Ollie-Pop.

POP!

"Whoa!" cried Gurdeep. "What's up with these bogus balloons?"

Ollie smiled to himself. Their plan was working.

Carlos and Sebastian darted forward and grabbed Ollie-Pops.

POP! POP!

"Are you thinking what I'm thinking?" Carlos asked Sebastian.

"You know it!" Sebastian replied. The brothers did a knuckle bump, scooped up handfuls of Ollie-Pops and took off running. The two boys dashed around the quad passing out Ollie-Pops to every kid holding a balloon.

The balloons began to pop slowly at first, like the sound of microwave popcorn as it starts to cook, eventually picking up steam and turning into to a full series of tiny explosions.

"Yeah, baby," hollered Carlos and Sebastian. The boys jumped in the air and double high-fived.

"Aubrey needs to get new balloons." Sebastian glanced around at the colorful scraps littering the blacktop. "These blow!"

Ollie silently congratulated himself on the smashing success of *Operation Pop Goes the Weasel*. It had taken Teddy several dozen tries, but he'd finally mastered the art of balloon-popping by way of his icy touch.

CHAPTER 13

NEW PROBLEM

"Did you see the look on her face?" Ollie said. "Aubrey just stood there with her head wobbling around like a bobble-head doll. Oh, so funny . . ." He finished with a sigh and wiped away the tears.

"Hysterical," Teddy said in a flat tone. "Look, we need to talk." He trotted alongside Ollie's bike.

"I know, I know." Ollie coasted to a stop and leaned his bike against the Bingham and Beans Building. "But first, I promised Captain Cook I'd bring the boxes back for recycling. While I'm here, I think I'll grab a scoop of rocky road." He finally noticed Teddy's cheerless face. "Sorry, dude. I wish you could throw back a cone."

"My inability to eat ice cream is the least of my worries." Teddy's brow furrowed and his dimples vanished.

"I know we need to talk, but can't I just enjoy the moment?" Ollie sighed. "I promise, we can talk later."

"You've got five minutes." With a frown and a glare, Teddy disappeared.

"Five minutes?" Ollie mumbled to himself. "By moment, I meant the rest of the day." For the first time in his life, he felt like he belonged. Deep down, he knew Teddy was about to burst his bubble—he could already feel the happiness seeping out of him one ounce at a time.

After dumping the boxes into the recycling bin, he strolled down the hill to the front door. A small cluster of kids from school greeted him with huge smiles and pats on the back.

"Nice blowout!" Carlos said, stepping aside to let him through.

Sebastian slung an arm around Ollie's shoulder and ushered him forward. "Someday, you gotta teach me that trick. It was totally awesome!"

"Hey, Ollie," Mikayla said softly. Her chestnut curls brushed past her cheek in loose spirals. "You were amazing!"

"Wow, thanks," Ollie said, feeling light-headed. "What's up?"

"We're here to get Ollie-Pops, of course." She tilted her head back and looked up at him, smiling. Her honey-brown eyes made his heart skip a beat. Ollie swallowed. His mind had turned to mush. Do. Not. Speak. He took a deep breath to slow his racing heart.

"Hey, Ollie!" Cole called out. "Over here."

Grateful for the interruption, Ollie swung around to find Cole sitting at a table next to the saltwater taffy. Teddy was perched on top of the ice cream freezer with his arms crossed. He pointed his chin at the clock on the wall. "Five minutes!"

Ollie pivoted away from Teddy and walked across the shop to speak with Cole. "Where's Gurdeep?" He rested one hand on the back of Cole's chair and slanted to one side in a casual stance. "I thought you guys were attached at the hip."

"At school," Cole said. "When I left, he was still slaving away at the Garden Project. I would have helped, but Miller said no can do."

With a sudden twinge of guilt, Ollie remembered it was because of him that Gurdeep was stuck with clean up duty. He'd been so busy with the campaign and the search for lost gold he'd forgotten all about Gurdeep's punishment. *I need to make that up to him.*

"I've never seen anything so funny," exclaimed Sebastian. "How'd ya do it? How'd ya pop the balloons?"

"Not sure how it happened." A sheepish smile tugged at Ollie's lips. "I guess it's a case of bad balloons."

"Riiight. Bad balloons," Carlos said, using air quotes. "If that's the story you wanna stick with, fine. But someday, you're gonna have to spill the beans."

Captain Cook came out from around the corner, carrying a tray of freshly made fudge. "Ahoy, matey! I heard you were a smashing success! In honor of your big day, I've added Ollie-Pops to the specials board."

"Cool." Ollie gazed around at his new friends. "I've never been a special anything."

"When you're done patting yourself on the back, we need to talk." Teddy paced back and forth now. "We've got a new problem."

Ollie lowered his head and whispered through clenched teeth, "I want to get a scoop of ice cream and hang out with my friends."

"Oh, I've got a scoop for you." Teddy frowned. "And, if rocky road is what you want, believe me, that's what you're about to get."

Ollie folded his arms across his chest and hissed, "Not leaving."

"Oh, yes you are." Teddy flicked a gummy bear at the back of Ollie's head.

"Fine!" Ollie burst out.

"Are you talking to me?" Mikayla asked, taking a timid step toward him.

"No-no," Ollie sputtered. "I was just thinking . . . What a fine day."

"Um, okay," Mikayla responded slowly, with a perplexed look on her face.

"Hey, guys, I'd love to hang out, but duty calls," Ollie announced to his friends. "Campaign stuff, ya know."

"Oh, fudge!" cried Carlos and Sebastian in unison.

"I know. I'm bummed too." Ollie stole a quick sidelong glance at Teddy. "I wish I could stay."

"No. Look!" Carlos pointed at the table in the center of the shop. "Captain Cook just put out a fresh plate of fudge."

"You thought they were bummed about you leaving," Teddy howled. "That's not embarrassing at all."

What a butthead. Ollie trudged toward the door. *Maybe he's a Kelly after all.*

"Do you have to go?" Mikayla touched his arm. "I was hoping we could have a soda or something."

"S-s-soda?" Ollie stammered. His heart pounded and his stomach fluttered. "I-I guess, well, maybe some other time?"

"Anytime." A smile danced across her heart-shaped lips. "Soon, I hope."

"Sounds good." Ollie backed up until he banged hard into the door. The bells sounded with a loud *clang.* "See ya." Spinning around, he yanked on the handle and made a hasty retreat.

"Smooth moves." Teddy chuckled. "You're quite the charmer."

"Whatever." Ollie grabbed the handlebars of his bike and started pushing it up the hill. Halfway up the steep incline, he paused to catch his breath. "So, what's got your suspenders in a bunch?"

Teddy's words tumbled out like a runaway train. "Mrs. Kelly. Five days. Bing closing—"

"Slow down, you sound like a chipmunk."

Teddy scowled and started over. "Mrs. Kelly bought Captain Cook's loan from the bank. She gave him a five-day notice to pay up. After that, it's lights out at the Bing!"

Like a fish out of water, Ollie's mouth dropped open, then closed, then open again. The news felt like a punch in the gut. He could see Teddy's lips moving, but all he could hear was a high-pitched ringing sound.

Whack!

A blast of cold air smacked Ollie upside the head.

"Snap out of it!" Teddy cried.

"Ow." Ollie rubbed the side of his face. "What'd you do that for?"

"Sorry." Teddy winced. "But you weren't listening. We need to make a new plan."

"Don't you get it?" Ollie cried. "It's over! This isn't some lame school election. This is real-life grown-up stuff. The only plan I'm making is how to survive another move."

"If we work together we can still find the gold."

"Unless you have a map with an X that marks the spot, we're done," Ollie replied in a thick voice.

Teddy spoke slowly and deliberately, as if talking to a small child. "Now, if you're going to be like that, I'll be forced to give you a time out. I am in no mood for your sarcasm."

"What I need is a time out from the crazy train I've been on ever since stepping foot in this town. Ghosts, bullies, campaigns, and long-lost gold. How much more am I sup-posed to take?"

"Now, hold your horses. I—"

Ollie jabbed an accusing finger at him. "Spooky Spratt. You did this to her. Now you're doing it to me."

"Are you done? If not, I'm more than happy to stop by later when you're not such a Negative Nelly. A positive atti-tude would be more helpful."

"Positive attitude? How's this? I'm positive you're out of your mind. I'm positive that by this time next week, I'll be on my way to Reno, Wichita, or Timbuktu."

"It doesn't have to be that way." Teddy pleaded. "We can do this."

Ollie's temper flared. "What's it matter to you? You're just a ghost. You have no idea what it feels like to be the odd man out, to never have any friends."

"I may be a ghost, but I've still got feelings." Teddy's mouth drew into a narrow line. "And for your information, I do know what it's like to be the odd man out, and I do know what it's like to not have any friends." He paused and glared at Ollie. "You're the best friend I've ever had—dead or alive. If you move, I'll be alone—again. At least you have your family. I don't have anyone."

A grim silence hung in the air.

"We can do this," Teddy said, breaking the silence. "I know we can."

"No, we can't." Ollie held up his palm to shut him up. "I'm not sure how much more I can take. I'm only twelve, and a very immature twelve, if you want to know the truth. It's over. We'll never find the gold. Leave me alone."

And right then and there, Ollie decided to come up with a new plan. One that did not involve a bothersome ghost.

CHAPTER 14

NEW 'DO

Ollie managed to get home before his eyes welled up, but he didn't let the tears fall. He threw his bike to the ground and flopped onto the grass in the shade of the lemon tree. In a blink, his newfound happiness was gone. He pictured leaving his new home, his new friends, and returning to a life of drifting from town to town.

This bleak turn of events left him feeling completely deflated. He sucked in a deep breath of air tinged with the tangy scent of lemons. His vision blurred, but this time, he let the tears flow. It seemed irrational, but man, he was really gonna to miss this tree.

A screech of brakes followed by the sound of tires crunching over gravel yanked him out of his pity party. Ollie jerked upright and wiped away his tears. Gurdeep was at the fence, doubled over, panting. His bike had been tossed aside as if he'd jumped off in a hurry.

"Dude." Ollie clambered to his feet and crossed the lawn. "You okay?" he asked, pushing aside his own concerns.

Gurdeep held up a finger to signal—just a second.

Far too many times, Ollie had been on the wrong end

of a chase. This bore all the signs of a kid on the lam. *Rule number one. When confronted by the enemy, employ evasive maneuvers.* He opened the gate and bent forward, glancing up and down the street. No sign of bad guys or buttheads. "Is someone after you?" he asked.

"No." Gurdeep waved his hand in the air, briefly pausing between words to catch his breath. "But you're about to get thrown out—"

"I know," Ollie interrupted. "Don't say it. It's just too depressing."

Gurdeep's flushed face went slack in confusion. "You know?" He arched an eyebrow and drew back. "How?"

Ollie hesitated a moment before answering. It's not like he could reveal his source. "Let's just say a little birdy told me." He rested a hand on Gurdeep's shoulder. "Like it or not, I am outta here."

"You're moving?" Gurdeep removed his helmet and wiped his sweaty brow.

"With the Bing closing, my mom's gonna have to find a new job. So . . ." His voice trailed off as he saw the look of relief on Gurdeep's face. "That's what you're talking about, right?"

For a split-second, it looked like Gurdeep was about to say something, but just as quickly, he appeared to change his mind. "Uh, yeah. Right," he replied, looking down at his hands. "That's what I was gonna say." Glancing up, he briefly made eye contact with Ollie, then his eyes slid away. "I'm sorry," he mumbled, his face turning a deep crimson red. "I mean it. I'm really sorry."

Ollie blinked away the tears that prickled his eyes. "Easy come. Easy go," he replied, shrugging. *Rule number two: Never let them see you sweat.* Shoving his hands into his pockets, he kicked at the gravel that lined Peach Street. "No biggie."

"Look, I-I-I really gotta go." Gurdeep abruptly clamped on his helmet and climbed back on his bike. Without saying another word, he shoved off and pedaled down the street at breakneck speed, as if he'd just remembered his favorite dinner was waiting for him at home.

As he disappeared around the corner, Ollie started to wonder about his visit. Was it his imagination or did Gurdeep seem like he was in some kind of trouble?

———

Hours later, Ollie kicked back on the couch, losing himself in reruns of *Scooby-Doo*. As usual, Shaggy and Scooby were scrambling to get away from a ghost. "You can run, but you can't hide," he grumbled, crunching down on a handful of popcorn.

Suddenly, DeeDee burst through the front door, extended her arms, and spun around in a circle. "I can fly, I can fly, I can fly!" she trilled, leaping onto the couch.

"Hey, watch it," Ollie said, snatching up his bowl of

popcorn before it tumbled onto the floor. Gus, lying at his feet, lifted his head and sniffed the air. Hank scampered across the room eager to snap up any stray kernels. "What's up with the new 'do?" he asked, eyeing her pixie haircut. "You look like a boy."

"I do?" DeeDee cried, in mock shock. "Maybe that's because I am a boy!" She vaulted off the couch and flew across the room, arms outstretched, giggling, until finally, slowing to a standstill and hugging herself. "You're looking at the new lead in the school play."

"Let me guess," he said, in a dull voice. "Peter Pan."

"That would be me!" she exclaimed, spinning like a top.

"Congrats." He managed a half-hearted smile. "I'm proud of you, sis." He thought of Teddy's news. *Oh, man, she's gonna be crushed.*

"All you need is faith, trust, and a little pixie dust," she chirped, bounding up the stairs two steps at a time with Hank nipping at her heels. "That, and a fab new 'do."

A few seconds later Mom strolled in, carrying a large pizza and a gold Cook's Candy box. "Celebratory dinner!" she announced holding the pizza box up in the air. "The Oxley family is on a roll. The Bing's season is almost sold out, we've got a star in the family, and Captain Cook told me you rocked the assembly." She beamed at Ollie. "I knew you could do it, kiddo."

Ollie felt his heart sink. The hits just kept on coming.

It was one thing to move when you were down and out. It was another thing entirely when everything was going your way. He'd never seen his family so happy. It was so unfair!

"Hello," Mom said, wafting the pizza box under his nose. "It's our favorite. Large Hawaiian. Extra pineapple. Extra cheese." The smell of cheesy goodness jolted him to his senses. Mom continued, "Now that I have your full attention, how about you go pick some lemons, and I'll make a batch of lemonade?"

"Sure." Ollie shrugged. "How many . . ." He stopped, a sudden thought crossed his mind. Something tugged at his memory. Something about lemons and fruit trees. And that's when it hit him. Why didn't he think of this before? "Mom! Remember when we first moved here? What was it you said about our neighborhood being a fruit orchard?"

"What?" Mom acted surprised, but genuinely pleased. "You were actually listening?"

Ollie rolled a hand impatiently. "Yeah. Yeah. When was it a fruit orchard?"

"Nice to see you taking an interest," she said, nodding her approval. "Our neighborhood was originally a fruit orchard in the 1800s."

"That's it!" Ollie cried. "Thanks, Mom."

It wasn't much. But maybe this new clue could help jog Teddy's one-hundred-fifty-year-old memory. Maybe it wasn't time to give up yet.

Ollie finally had friends and a place that actually felt like home. If the Kellys thought he was going down without a fight, they were wrong. Dead wrong! There was no way he planned on implementing rule number three: *If rules one and two fail—run for your life.*

All I need is faith, trust, and a little pixie dust, and maybe, just maybe, a bothersome ghost.

CHAPTER 15
NEW TRICK

Teddy stood at Miss Sally's door, summoning the courage to face his past. *I can do this*, he thought, determined to make things right. *I should knock. I don't want to scare the bejeebers out of her.* Squaring his shoulders, he knocked on the door three times for good luck.

"Who's there?" Miss Sally called out in a cheerful voice.

"Teddy," he said using his best aren't-you-happy-to-see-me voice.

"Teddy who?" she replied in a not-so-cheerful voice.

"Teddy the ghost."

Silence . . . More silence . . . Dead silence.

Teddy heard the clinking of a chain, then the loud click of the deadbolt. Slowly, the door squeaked open. Miss Sally peeked out through the narrow crack. Seconds passed as she gazed at the blond-haired, blue-eyed boy standing on her porch.

"Hey, long time, no see," Teddy said, with a slight wave of his hand.

BAM!

She slammed the door in his face.

Hmm, interesting. Not so bad—at least she didn't yell.

Teddy decided to make himself at home on the porch swing. Apparently, Miss Sally needed a few minutes to gather her thoughts. Maybe splash cold water on her face. Have a cup of hot tea? Everything would be okay.

With great fondness, he remembered the first time he'd met her. Sally was twelve. She and her best friend, Edna, were playing hide-and-seek. While Edna counted to ten, Sally ran to the backyard to hide behind the woodshed. Even though no one could see him, he decided to play along. Taking cover, he hid behind a large hydrangea bush not far from Sally's hiding spot.

"That plant isn't nearly big enough to hide you," she whispered. "Edna's gonna spot you the second she comes around the corner. Quick, come hide with me."

Teddy's jaw dropped. *She can see me!*

"Are you deaf?" she said. "I don't know who you are; either move it or lose it!"

Before he could respond, Edna came flying around the corner and ran straight past him to the woodshed. "Found ya! If you don't want me to find you, then maybe you shouldn't talk to yourself."

Sally's face turned a bright shade of rosy red. She spun around to give Teddy a piece of her mind. "Thanks a—"

With a twinkle in his eye and a dimpled grin, he disappeared.

Teddy kicked his legs back and forth, lost in thought. The sound of the front door opening snapped him back to the present. Miss Sally poked her head out. "You'd better come inside. I don't want to be seen talking to myself. It's taken me thirty years to live down the name Spooky Spratt."

"They still . . ." Teddy's voice trailed off. "No. Never mind." He hopped off the swing and followed her inside. Out of habit, he stopped to wipe his feet on the mat. Sometimes he just plain forgot he was a ghost.

Miss Sally settled in on the sofa. "So you're back? Did you forget something? Like, um, I don't know, goodbye? You promised to meet me after school. You left me all alone. Spooky Spratt, the girl with no friends."

"I thought it was the right thing to do," Teddy apologized. "Edna made your life miserable. I hated that she called you Spooky Spratt. If I coulda shut her down, I woulda. But I couldn't, so I went away."

Silence.

"I handled it wrong," Teddy murmured. "I'm sorry."

A tear rolled down Miss Sally's cheek. "Oh drat! I could never stay mad at you for long. I'm just so darned happy to see you." She reached for a tissue and blew her nose long and hard. "So, tell me, what kind of shenanigans are you up to now?"

"Well, I hate to tell you this, but Edna Kelly is still causing problems," Teddy said. Pacing back and forth, he brought

Miss Sally up to speed, spelling out the details of Mrs. Kelly's plans to shut down Cook's Candy and the Bing.

"So Edna is up to her old tricks," Miss Sally said, with an exaggerated sigh.

"Yes. But this time, I have a new trick up my sleeve. This time, Edna's not going to win." Teddy pounded his fist on the coffee table so hard it sent tiny ripples through Miss Sally's tea. "We need to find my pa's gold and save the day."

"Are you referring to the gold we spent an entire summer looking for?" Miss Sally arched an eyebrow and pursed her lips.

"Yes," Teddy exclaimed. "But this time, I know where to look. Thanks to a photograph you found."

"Count me in!" declared Miss Sally. "Wait a minute. What photograph? Have you been spying on me?"

Teddy vigorously shook his head. "No! Never. So wrong!"

Miss Sally gave him the side-eye.

"Yes." Teddy gave a half-hearted shrug and weak smile. "Yes, I have."

CHAPTER 16
NEW MISSION

Ollie's room looked like a tornado had just touched down. The floor was a maze of books and papers and little heaps of dirty laundry. Every dresser drawer was open and the contents spilled out onto the floor. Board games, shoes, and sports equipment trickled out of the closet.

He had turned everything upside down and inside out, searching for his math test. He still needed to have his mom sign it. With a deep exhale of resignation, he threw himself on the floor, closed his eyes, and tried to picture where he'd seen it last.

"If this is packing, you're not very good at it," Teddy commented. "Which is surprising, considering how many times you've moved."

Ollie's eye flew open and he bolted upright. "Finally! It's about time you showed up. Where've you been?"

"So you're talking to me again?" Teddy dropped down on the floor next to him.

"About that." Ollie toyed with a pair of dice from a board game, avoiding eye contact. "I'm sorry I yelled at you. I've been so caught up in my own problems I never stopped to think about how you were feeling." He drew a shaky breath, then continued, "Still friends?"

"Aw, shucks." Teddy broke out into a big, cheeky grin. "It was just a dust-up between two amigos. Forget about it. We ain't got no time to waste on such nonsense. My pa's gold ain't gonna find itself."

"Thanks, dude." Ollie tossed the dice against the wall, rolling snake-eyes. "I've been giving this a lot of thought, and I'm not about to let Aubrey win."

"Sounds like somebody decided to man up," Teddy remarked with a satisfied nod. "Which is very good news because we've got help."

"Really?" Ollie's mind raced with scary possibilities. "Please don't tell me you've summoned a miner forty-niner."

"Very funny." Teddy smirked. "Actually, I've recruited Miss Sally."

"Oh, yeah? How did that blast from the past go?"

"A little bumpy." Teddy grimaced. "But after a while she warmed up to me. I can be quite charming when I put my mind to it," he added, polishing his knuckles on his shirt.

"Did you fess up about shaking tables for street cred? And the fact that she's *not* a medium?"

"Yes, and I can assure you, she was not too pleased." Teddy sighed. "But now that I've cleared the air and apologized, she has agreed to help us find the gold."

"Awesome. We can use all the help we can get," Ollie said,

rolling onto his side and peering under the bed for his math test. There was nothing there except a sock and Gus's favorite chew toy. Grabbing the rubber bone, he tossed it to his dog. Gus wagged his tail and padded over to investigate. Sniffing the bone, he nudged it with his muzzle, then snapped it up and dashed out of the room.

"Weird. I just realized something," Ollie said. "Gus doesn't bark at you anymore."

"Yeah, well, like I said, I can be quite charming." Teddy waved him off and kept talking. "I have news. Big news. I found a new clue. I would have told you yesterday if you hadn't thrown such a hissy fit and stormed off."

"Whatever." Ollie sulked. "It's not like you're the one who has to move."

"You're not moving! That's what I've been trying to tell you."

"Did you really find a new clue?" Ollie asked, anxious to share his own newly discovered clues.

"I did, and it's a whopper." Teddy leaned in close and spoke in a hushed tone. "Miss Sally found a photograph of my family. When I saw it, I remembered something. The picture was taken on the very day my pa struck gold. A photographer from the *Granite City Gazette* took a picture of my family in front of our house. Later, that same day, my pa hid the gold for safekeeping. He buried it next to a tree behind my house. All we need to do is find my house, find that tree, and dig."

Ollie gave a noncommittal grunt. "Say we do find your house, am I just supposed to knock on the door and say, 'Hey, you don't know me, but can I dig a hole in your backyard? Oh, P. S., if I find a crap-load of gold, do you mind if I keep it?'"

"We'll cross that bridge when we get to it."

Ollie tugged at his eyebrow.

"Ya know . . ." Teddy cringed. "You may want to lay off the eyebrow. It's looking a little sparse."

"I'm trying." Ollie stroked what was left of his eyebrow. "How do you know the gold is still there?"

"I know it is!" Teddy exclaimed. "My pa passed away from pneumonia a few months after he buried the gold. I'm the only other person who knew about it. Once we figure out where I lived, we'll come up with a plan to dig."

"I have a couple new clues too," Ollie began. He felt a tad uneasy about sharing his news about Aubrey Kelly. Clearing his throat, he forged ahead. "Yesterday, at assembly, I noticed a plaque nailed to the trunk of the oak tree. The thing is—"

"I knew it," Teddy exclaimed. "I knew you were acting strange about something."

"Let me finish. The plaque was dedicated to Martin K. Kelly, some rich dude who donated land to the city. Does that name ring a bell?"

"Martin K. Kelly?" Teddy's eyes bugged out. "As in Aubrey Kelly?"

"Bingo!" Ollie tapped his nose then pointed his finger at Teddy. "I think we need to consider the real possibility that you may be a Kelly."

"Ewww." Teddy blurred like a picture out of focus. "If that's true, and I seriously hope it isn't, we need Miss Sally's help now more than ever. We can ask her to look into the Kelly family tree."

"Good thinking," Ollie said, getting back into the spirit of the treasure hunt.

"What's your second clue?" Teddy asked. "I hope it's not as disgusting as your last one."

"Fruit orchard," Ollie blurted out, searching Teddy's face for any sign of recognition.

"You mean Farmer McMullen's fruit orchard?" Teddy asked, rubbing the side of his head. "Wait a minute . . ." he said, drawing out the words. "I can't believe I just remembered that."

"What else do you remember?" Ollie asked, his body tingling with excitement.

"I remember his tasty peaches!" Teddy's licked his lips. "Eli and I used to sneak into his orchard to steal peaches and lemons and persimmons," he said with a faraway look in his eyes. "And figs for my ma!"

"What else?"

"I remember . . ."

"Yes?" Ollie leaned in so close to Teddy he caught a chill.

"From my house, I had to walk through the orchard to get to my favorite fishing hole. On the way, I'd always nick a peach or persimmon to take with me."

"The same fishing hole that was ruined when they built the bridge?"

Teddy smiled. "That's the one."

"That would mean your house was on this side of the river!" Ollie exclaimed. "You just cut our search area in half!" He grabbed a piece of paper off the floor and riffled through his junk for a pen. "Let's list our clues. Then we can figure out where to go next." He clicked his pen and wrote:

The Search For Lost Gold

1. Teddy's last name begins with a K.

2. Teddy: Possibly a Kelly

3. Gold buried behind Teddy's house, next to a tree.

4. Teddy's house is on this side of the river.

"I really think we can do this," Ollie said, reviewing the clues.

"I know we can." Teddy slammed his fist into the palm of his hand.

"The clock is ticking," Ollie said. "It's time we find us some gold!"

"Eureka!" Teddy punched the air in triumph. "We have a new mission: Operation Gold Rush."

CHAPTER 17
NEW LOW

It was election day. Ollie hoped the bad weather was not a sign of things to come. A drop of rain landed on his nose and trickled down onto his lip. He wiped it away and tilted his head skyward. Thunder rumbled in the distance. Electricity charged the air. A storm was coming.

Ollie picked up the pace as the rain started to fall in a light drizzle. Lightning flashed, followed by a rolling crash of thunder. He jogged down the street, holding his backpack over his head. More kids fell in step with him, racing for cover. Big drops of rain were falling by the time he reached Suds. One unlucky kid got stuck holding the door open as students poured inside. Slowing to a walk, Ollie pulled out of the main flow of traffic and checked his phone for messages.

DeeDee: *Hope you win!*

Mom: *Proud of you! oooxxx*

"Hey, bro." Cole gave him a friendly thump on the back. "You got this thing in the bag."

"Thanks." Ollie shook the water off his backpack. "I guess we'll know soon enough." Clutching his cell phone, he checked the time. "Oh, man. We're gonna be late."

The two boys sprinted down the hall. Halfway to class, a pack of girls blocked their path. Cole screeched to a full stop in front of a redhead and slid in next to her. "Hey, Brooke, how you doing?"

Ollie kept going. *It wouldn't look good for the new class president to be late.* Taking a hard right at the end of the hall, he bumped into Aubrey, who was stationed in front of homeroom.

"Oh, you're still here?" she sneered, smugness seeping out of every pore.

"Where else would I—"

"Oliver Oxley!" Mr. Miller walked briskly toward him. He did not look or sound happy. As a matter of fact, he looked downright angry. "Principal's office. Now!" he ordered, handing him a detention slip. "Mr. Ritter is expecting you."

"Wait! What? Why? What'd I do?" Ollie stammered, his head spinning. Students brushed past with curious glances, several lingered to gawk and snicker.

Mr. Miller seethed like a simmering pot of stew ready to boil over. "I think you know."

"I don't—"

"Save it for Mr. Ritter." Mr. Miller turned his back on him, unlocked the door to homeroom and went inside.

"Oi! Somebody's in trouble." Aubrey snickered. "And it's not me," she added before disappearing into class.

Ollie scanned the pink slip for clues. Under the heading

Policy Violation, Mr. Miller had checked the box marked Destruction of School Property. *Pink house? Pink detention slip? Ugh! Pink does not make me happy.*

The second bell rang, leaving students scrambling to get to class and the hall quickly emptied.

Cole flew around the corner and charged down the hall. "Bro, what'd ya do?" he asked, eyeballing the detention slip.

"Dunno. Maybe it's got something to do with my math test. I forgot to have it signed."

"Bro, you must've really bombed," Cole said, taking a step back as if he didn't want to catch the detention bug. "Bitter Ritter's the worst."

"Awesome. I feel so much better." Ollie's head pounded like a jackhammer in a construction zone. "See ya."

"See ya, bro." Cole slipped into homeroom. "Or not."

For a brief moment, Ollie heard the familiar sound of papers rustling and textbooks opening. Then the door closed with a final click, and all was quiet. A feeling of gloom settled into the pit of his stomach. He replayed the events of the last couple days in his mind like the highlights reel of a football game. Nothing criminal came to mind. Well, almost nothing. *Do they know about Teddy? Can I get in trouble for conspiring with a ghost?*

The only sound in the empty corridor was the squeaking of his sneakers against the tile floor. He dragged his feet to slow down time. The principal's office loomed ominously at the end of the hall. His heart hammered in his ears. It grew louder with each step. An eighth-grade hall monitor trolled the corridor in search of tardy students. "You there!" he yelled. "Where's your hall pass?"

Ollie flashed his pink detention slip.

"Dead man walking." The monitor whipped out his phone and snapped a picture of Ollie. "Wannabe class prez hits the skids on election day." He snickered. "Hashtag LOSER."

Ollie managed a thin smile. "Gee. Thanks." He froze at the office door. His knuckles turned white as he gripped the doorknob. Assuming his best I'm-innocent face, he walked into the danger zone.

A petite woman with spiky black hair and sharp features was camped out behind the large laminate desk. Her gaze remained fixed on the computer screen. "Take a seat. There are two people ahead of you," she said over the whir of a photocopier.

Ollie craned his neck to get a better view of the principal's office through the window in his door. Cinda and Sierra were sitting very prim and proper with their backs to him. Mr. Ritter appeared to be listening intently with a grave expression etched across his face.

What's going on? Ollie lowered himself into a chair, one eye trained on the gargoyles. The ripped vinyl seat snagged the seam of his shorts and the fluorescent lighting made his head hurt.

As the minutes slowly ticked by, his sense of dread grew exponentially. The telephone rang, kids came and went. The secretary clicked away at her keyboard. He tugged at his eyebrow and counted ceiling tiles. When Mr. Ritter's door finally opened, Sierra and Cinda emerged with victorious grins plastered to their mugs.

"Have a nice vacation, Oxley." Cinda smirked.

"Yeah, don't be a stranger," Sierra added. "Wait, on second thought they don't come much stranger than you. Later, loser."

The gargoyles exited the office in a cloud of giggles and smirks.

"Ouch," Teddy exclaimed. "What's up with Poo and Doo?"

Ollie flinched. "It's about time you got here," he whispered out the side of his mouth.

"Sorry. I was meeting with Miss Sally about Operation Gold Rush. What's up?"

"Not sure, but I don't have a good feeling."

"Mr. Oxley, you may come in now." Mr. Ritter's voice came through the open door.

Ollie rose from his chair at the same time his mom entered the office, appearing slightly frazzled. Her blonde hair was pulled back in a messy ponytail, and her eyes were red and puffy. Water dripped from her umbrella.

"Uh-oh." Teddy grimaced. "That can't be good." With a shrug and a frown, he disappeared.

"Hey, Mom," Ollie said in an uneasy tone. "What are you doing here?"

"I guess we're about to find out." She blew a damp wisp of hair out of her eyes and tucked her hands under her elbows. "This is the last thing I need today."

"Sorry, Mom. I've no idea what's going on."

"Just go." She nudged him toward the principal's office.

Ollie followed his mom into the cramped office. He looked around the room. Floor-to-ceiling shelves covered the walls, jam-packed with books, binders, and framed awards. Rain pelted down outside the window. A crack of lightning washed the room with a sudden burst of light, casting a spotlight on a grizzled old man with silver hair and steely-gray eyes. "Please, take a seat." He gestured toward the two chairs in front of his desk.

Ollie glanced at Mr. Ritter's desk. It was a sea of paperwork. At the center of the clutter, he spotted his math test. *Whew, that explains everything.* Mom folded herself onto the chair. Ollie parked himself on the same chair that Cinda had occupied only moments ago. It was still warm. *Gross.* He scooched to the edge.

"Thank you for coming, Mrs. Oxley," Mr. Ritter said. "I'm sorry to meet under such unpleasant circumstances."

"Look, I can explain," Ollie said. "I'm sorry about my math test. I know I should've had it signed, like, last week but I lost it. I didn't know it was such a big deal."

Mr. Ritter's bushy eyebrows furrowed together like two angry caterpillars facing off in a grudge match. "Oliver, this has nothing to do with your math test. We know you destroyed the class garden."

"What the—"

"Please don't try to deny it." Mr. Ritter held up his hand to silence him. "We found your math test at the scene, and we have two eyewitnesses who've said that it was you who destroyed the garden."

The news hit Ollie like a ton of fertilizer. Aubrey had set him up, and boy did it stink. *Wow. She must seriously want to be class president. This is a whole new low, even for her.* He looked to his mom for support. "Mom?" She chewed on her lower lip as if to fight back tears. "Mom?" he repeated, feeling a lump in his throat.

"Oh, right." Mom shook her head clear. "Oliver, why would two people say they saw you destroy the garden? Why would they make that up?"

"Because Cinda and Sierra are Aubrey's lackeys," Ollie cried, anger burning through him. "Why would I destroy the garden? Things are going great. I think I might even win the election."

"Correction, Mr. Oxley. You're disqualified," said Mr. Ritter. "As of now, you're suspended for ten days." Turning back to Mom, he asked, "Mrs. Oxley, is there anything you'd like to add?"

"No." Her shoulders dropped in resignation. "I'm sorry to have troubled you."

"That's it?" Bitterness bubbled up in Ollie's throat. "You're not going to defend me?"

"Oliver, get your things, we're going home." She pushed herself out of the chair. "We'll discuss this later."

Wait! What? This is crazy! Ollie seethed at the unfairness of it. He opened his mouth to argue then closed it again. Why bother? It was obvious that he'd already been tried, convicted, and sentenced for a crime he did not commit. He stood abruptly and ran out the door.

———————————

Mom broke the silence as they pulled to a stop in their driveway. "Oliver, you've done a lot of crazy things, but this is by far the worst. You're officially grounded for life."

"I didn't do it!" Ollie protested. "How can you even believe I would do something so horrible? Have I done some stupid things? Sure. But never anything like this." He waited, arms folded, expecting an apology.

Mom stared straight ahead. She sighed, but said nothing.

"Thanks a lot for your awesome support." Ollie bolted out of the car and stormed up the front walk. He kicked the red doormat off the porch and wrenched the door open, slamming it shut behind him.

Teddy was sitting on top of the armoire, swishing his

legs from side to side like a windshield wiper. "Grounded for life? That seems a bit harsh."

"I know, right? It's totally unfair." Ollie pushed his bedroom door open.

"Just out of curiosity, what does grounded for life mean?" Teddy hopped down and followed him into the room. "It sounds painful."

Ollie threw himself on the bed and stared at the ceiling. "It means I'm not allowed to leave the house."

"Never ever again? For the rest of your life? Can she do that?"

"No. Of course not. I'll be out in two weeks with time off for good behavior." Ollie wrestled off his shoes. "So I might as well get comfortable."

"What about Operation Gold Rush?" Teddy panicked. "How are we going to find the gold when you're stuck at home?"

"I never said I'd follow the rules of lockdown. Tomorrow, after my mom leaves for work, we'll meet up at Miss Sally's."

"That's the spirit!"

———————

A short time later, there was a soft tap at the door. DeeDee poked her head inside. "I brought you dinner." She bumped the door open with her shoulder and walked into the room carrying a plate of hot dogs and beans. Hank waddled in after her and curled up next to Gus.

Ollie swung his legs around and sat up on the edge of his bed. "Thanks." He eyed his meal. "Prison food?"

"Ha, ha," DeeDee murmured in a flat tone. Handing him the plate, she dropped down on the bed next to him and gently bopped his shoulder with hers. "I know you didn't do it. Deep down, Mom does, too."

"It doesn't feel that way," Ollie garbled with a mouth full of beans. "A little support would've been nice when I was getting thrown under the bus."

"Don't be mad," DeeDee said, her voice cracking. "Mom had a really bad day. I think we're moving again."

"I know." Ollie put the plate down on his dresser and slung an arm around her shoulders. "Maybe something will turn up." He sounded more confident than he felt. He was surprised to see her so upset at the thought of moving. She was usually so happy to go with the flow, wherever that might take them. "I thought you liked to move," he said softly, and then, in a high-pitched, theatrical voice, he added, "I thought moving was a big adventure."

"I'm a better actor than you think." Tears trickled down her cheek. "I miss having a home, like a real home, one that we don't leave." She swiped her face with the palm of her hand. "And I miss Dad."

"Me, too." Ollie gave her shoulder a quick squeeze. "But he's not coming back. It's just the three of us now. We're family, and families stick together. Hang in there, sis. It's not over till it's over. Or, as you like to say, until the fat lady sings."

"You hang in there, too." DeeDee sniffed. "Hopefully tomorrow Mom will have a change of heart."

CHAPTER 18

NEW CLUE

Morning sunlight streamed in through the window. The storm had blown over. Ollie wiped the crust from his eyelids and the drool from his chin. Dragging himself out of bed, he threw on some clothes and stumbled half-asleep to the kitchen. Gus padded after him, wagging his tail.

Mom pushed away from the counter as he walked into the room. An angry expression clouded her features. "You may eat and do homework. No TV. No Xbox. No leaving the house." She gulped down the last dregs of coffee and reached for her keys. "Got it?"

"Got it. I'll do the time for my imaginary crime."

"Good," Mom said, ignoring his sarcasm. And then she made a squishy face as if fighting back an avalanche of tears. "Sweetie," she said, softening her tone. "There's something I need to tell you." She fidgeted with her keys. "Captain Cook may lose his building, which means . . ."

"Which means, we may have to move again," Ollie whispered. "I know."

"I'm sorry." Mom made the squishy face again. "Maybe he'll find a way to get the money. In the meantime, I still have a job to do." Slinging her purse over her shoulder she leaned on the banister and yelled, "DeeDee! Time to go!"

DeeDee flew down the stairs with Hank by her side. At the bottom of the steps, she paused in front of the hall mirror, brushed her bangs out of her eyes, and applied a thin layer of pink lip gloss. "Ready!" She grabbed her backpack off the counter. "Try not to burn the house down, Prison Boy."

"Whatever, DoDo," Ollie fired back. So much for their kumbaya moment last night. "Don't let the door hit your butt on the way out."

"Stop!" Mom cried. "Just this once, can you two get along? I have enough on my plate without the two of you bickering like a pair of alley cats."

"I'm pretty sure alley cats don't bicker," Ollie mumbled. "More like fight or caterwaul."

"I'll pretend I didn't hear that." Mom spun around on her heels and marched down the hall. Ollie traipsed after her, mentally shooing her out the door. As Mom clutched the doorknob, she turned and stared him down. "Please. Stay out of trouble."

"I will," he promised, crossing his fingers behind his back.

"I mean it." She sighed. "One more slip-up and you're done." With one last devastating glare, she walked out the door, DeeDee in tow. The Mom Bomb hung in the air like a dark cloud: gloomy and foreboding. Ollie didn't know what she meant by 'done,' but it didn't sound good. He ran to the window and watched her back the car down the driveway, pull onto Peach Street, and disappear from view.

Grabbing his backpack, he raced across the street to Miss Sally's, splashing in puddles along the way. At her fence, he unlatched the gate, pushed it open, and trekked up the front walk. As usual, Teddy was making himself at home on the porch swing. "Ollie's here!" he bellowed at the top of his lungs.

Ollie quickly covered his ears with his hands. "Dude, I could've done that." He glared from the bottom of the stairs. "You almost blew out my eardrums."

Teddy chuckled. "She'll be out in a minute."

Miss Sally opened the door with one hand while balancing an armload of books with the other. Ollie climbed the steps and rushed over to help. "Here, let me get that," he offered, scooping up the stack of books before they tumbled to the ground.

"Thank you," Miss Sally said gratefully, sitting down on the front stoop.

Ollie plopped down next to her and waited while she arranged the books. When she was done earmarking several pages, she spoke, "I understand I have you to thank for this one's sudden return to my life." She cocked an eyebrow and tilted her head in Teddy's direction.

"No problem," Ollie said. "He never should have left you hanging."

"I know. How hard is it to say goodbye?"

"Or leave a note. He's really good at messages."

"True." Miss Sally leveled her gaze at Teddy. "If he can shake a table, he most certainly can leave a note."

"No kidding." Ollie gave Teddy the stink-eye.

"I suppose I've always known I wasn't a medium," she added with a wistful smile.

Ollie made a *tsk-tsk* sound and shook his head. "Bad, ghost!"

"Hey, wait a minute—" Teddy's face registered surprise and indignation.

Ollie gave a dismissive flick of his hand and continued, "When you guys hung out, did he always laugh at his own jokes?"

"You mean like, 'What does a ghost serve for dessert?'"

"'I-scream.'" Ollie groaned. "Seriously. Not funny."

Teddy's head volleyed back and forth between his two friends as they spoke.

"Does he appear out of nowhere when you least expect it, making you look like a complete fool?" asked Miss Sally.

"Like, every day." Ollie nodded. "Have you ever played hangman with him? 'Cause if you have, you know he's a total cheat."

"Hellooo," Teddy cut in. "I'm right here."

"I know," Miss Sally said, shaking her head. "Smarty pants used to make up words all the time."

"Hey, guys." Teddy raised his hand and pointed a finger at himself. "I'm sitting right here. I can hear you. I may be a ghost, but I know you can see me."

"Oh, Teddy, you know we love you," Miss Sally said with a bemused twinkle in her eye.

"Love is a strong word," Ollie teased. "I'm thinking more along the lines of tolerate."

"I'm glad to see you're both so amused at my expense." Teddy sniffed. "Maybe we should get to work. Time's running out."

"You're right," Miss Sally said. "Time to put on our thinking caps."

"Did you find the copy of the *Granite City Gazette* my family was featured in?" Teddy raised his eyebrows and offered a questioning gaze.

"No," Miss Sally replied. "I've been searching the newspaper archives to no avail. If the story about your family was in one of the earliest editions, there might not be a record. In the meantime, we need to search for new clues." She reached over and pulled out a large binder from her pile of books. She propped it up on her lap and flipped through the pages until she found the one she wanted. "This is a copy of the photograph of you and your family. The original is hanging at the museum."

Ollie scooched in closer to Miss Sally and studied the photograph. The snapshot was of a family sitting on a front porch. Teddy's mother and father were seated rigidly in chairs. Teddy and Eli were sitting on the stoop at their feet. All four sat stony-faced. "Teddy, why isn't anyone smiling? Your dad just struck it rich. You should be grinning from ear to ear."

Teddy peered over Miss Sally's shoulder. "In my day, getting your picture taken was a solemn occasion. It was nothing like the look-at-me, selfie world you live in today. Plus, the way cameras worked back then, taking a picture could take hours. It's hard to hold a smile for that long, even for me."

Ollie had never given much thought to what it was like to live in the 1800s. No television. No computer. No paved roads. No cars. No cell phones. *Yikes!*

Miss Sally held up a magnifying glass and moved it slowly over the image. "This photo doesn't provide much help." She knitted her eyebrows together. "It's too bad it's such a tight shot. I wish we could see more of the house," she added. "Most of the homes in this part of Granite City have front porches just like this."

"So we have nothing new to go on." Ollie slumped forward and sighed.

"Let's see if we can find anything in here." Miss Sally thumbed through the pages of a book titled *The Guide to*

Historical Homes of Granite City. She compared each historic home to the picture of Teddy's house.

"Nothing." Miss Sally closed the book and placed it on her lap. "Teddy, I think you need to look for a landmark or something that may seem familiar to you. That might be our only chance of finding a new clue."

"Is there anything else you can remember about where you lived?" Ollie asked. "A big rock, a tree, anything?"

"No. Nothing." Teddy gazed anxiously at his friends. "Back in my day, there wasn't much here except for dirt and more dirt."

"Have you been able to find out anything about Martin Kelly?" Ollie wondered.

"I have." Miss Sally leafed through the pages of a notebook until she found a copy of an old newspaper article. "I found this *Granite City Gazette* story on microfilm, dated June twenty-eighth, eighteen ninety-nine. It's an interview with Martin Kelly on the very day he donated five acres of land to the city."

"What's it say?" Teddy peered at her with interest.

"Most of the story is not pertinent to our search. However, there is one bit of useful information. In the article, Mr. Kelly said that he owes all of his good fortune to his grandfather, William Kelly, a prospector who struck it rich during the Gold Rush."

"Does the name William Kelly ring a bell?" Ollie regarded Teddy with nervous apprehension. "Could he be your dad?"

"William Kelly . . . William Kelly . . . William Kelly." The name rolled off Teddy's tongue as if trying it on for size. "It does have a familiar ring to it, but to me, my father was just Pa."

"Can you find a picture of William Kelly?" Ollie asked. "Then we'll know for sure if he was Teddy's dad."

"I'll try," Miss Sally replied. "But, Teddy, if you think there's a possibility that William Kelly was your father, we need to find out where he lived. In the meantime, I think you boys should go house to house. Maybe Teddy will stumble upon something that rings a bell. I'll continue my research while you boys are gone."

"Agreed." Teddy nodded.

"Agreed." Ollie followed suit.

"Then it's settled." Miss Sally snapped her notebook shut. "I'll go to work. You boys need to get going. If you find a new clue, let me know. Don't do anything crazy, like dig up someone's backyard."

"Gotcha." Ollie gave a Boy Scout salute.

"Yes, ma'am." Teddy put his dimples on full display.

Minutes later, the two boys headed down the street. Ollie charted a course of action using the map Miss Sally gave him. "I'll mark off each street as we go. You keep your eyes peeled for anything that looks familiar."

"Who put you in charge?" Teddy demanded. "This is *my* plan."

"Yeah, well, you're a ghost, so I'm in charge." Ollie continued walking with his nose buried in the map.

"Stop!" Teddy screamed, coming to a halt in front of a blue Victorian. "This place feels familiar. Stay here, I'll take a peek inside."

Before Ollie could object, Teddy disappeared. *Ugh! I hate it when he does that.*

A moment later a shrill scream shattered the morning calm on Peach Street.

Teddy reappeared, a bit rattled. "I guess you and Miss Sally aren't the only two people in town who can see ghosts." He shoved his hands into his pocket and moved quickly down the street. "I sure hope she's gonna be okay," Teddy mumbled, eyes darting back at the house. "I gave her quite a fright. And nothing inside the house looked familiar to me."

"She'll be fine," Ollie assured, uncertainty crossing his face. "Let's keep moving."

———————

Four hours later, Ollie stared at the map, trying to decide where to go next. So far, the only thing they had succeeded in doing was scaring the heck out of some poor grandma.

"If we continue down Persimmon Street, we'll hit Apple Avenue. There, I think we should go left and then circle back and end up here," Ollie said, tapping the map.

"Apple Avenue?" Teddy perked up. "That reminds me of another joke."

"No!" Ollie cried. "No more fruit jokes, plea—"

"When is an apple a grouch?" Teddy asked, bobbing his eyebrows up and down.

Ollie gave him the slow blink. "I. Don't. Know. Maybe when the apple is best friends with a ghost?"

"Wrong!" Teddy faced Ollie and walked backward. "When it's a crab apple. Get it? Crab apple!"

"Got it." Ollie favored him with a blank stare. "You're not helping," he added, taking a deep breath to calm his nerves. A feeling of panic was beginning to settle in. His whole body puckered with tension.

The expression on Teddy's face shifted from amusement to concern. "Sorry, I was just trying to lighten the mood." He flipped back around and fell in step with Ollie. "I wish I could picture things like they used to be. Like I said—"

"That's it." Ollie stopped and stared at Teddy. "You *can* picture it! We need to go to the museum. They have a million pictures!" He shoved the map into his backpack and took off running. "Come on!"

"Pictures?" Teddy chased after him. "I love pictures!"

When the two boys arrived at the town center, Ollie looked up and down the street to make sure his mom was nowhere in sight. The last thing he needed was to run into her while she was on a coffee break or out for a stroll. All clear. Quickly, he sprinted down the sidewalk and ducked into the museum entrance. Reaching into his pocket, he pulled out a five dollar bill. "Two please," he said to the lady at the ticket counter.

"Two?" she questioned, craning her neck out the window.

Teddy chuckled.

"Er, I mean one." Ollie drew his mouth into a tight line. "Thanks." He accepted the change and the ticket and went inside. "This museum is covered with pictures from the 1800s," he told Teddy as they made their way through the maze of rooms. "One of these old photos is bound to jog your memory."

"You mean like this one?" Teddy pointed at a grainy photograph of an old Victorian and began reading the caption. "Kelly House—Built 1850. In 1899 Martin K. Kelly donated his ancestral home and the surrounding five acres to Granite City. In 1901 the Kelly House was torn down to make way for Sudbury Middle School. Kelly Hall now stands in the exact location of where the Kelly House once stood." Teddy paused to let the news sink in. "I think we found our new clue."

Ollie felt the color drain from his face.

"Maybe the reason we can't find my house is because it no longer exists." Teddy explained, picking up the pace of his words. "Maybe—"

"Don't say it!" Ollie smacked his forehead and groaned. "Please, don't say it."

"The gold was buried at school. Based on the location of Kelly Hall, my best guess is that it was buried in the quad by the oak tree!" Teddy exclaimed. "Hot diggity dog!"

"Nuts," Ollie muttered. "Just when I thought things couldn't get any worse."

CHAPTER 19
NEW BATTERIES

"**D**o you think the bandana is really necessary?" Teddy settled back onto the beanbag chair and crossed his arms. "You look like a bandit."

Ollie tugged at the black scarf that covered half his face. "Yes. I do. I'm in enough trouble as it is. The last thing I need is my mug captured on the school security cam."

"I told you. There are no cameras pointed at the quad. Relax."

"Easy for you to say. If I get caught, I get expelled. If you get caught—oh, wait—you can't get caught. You're a ghost."

"You won't get caught. Not with me as your lookout. Grab your flashlight."

Ollie glanced at the clock radio. It was almost midnight. Mom and DeeDee were finally asleep. He too should be fast asleep like a normal kid, but he wasn't normal. His best friend was a ghost, and he was about to dig for buried treasure at his middle school. Which he was currently suspended from.

Game time. He reached under his bed, pulled out the flashlight and thumbed it on. The light flickered and went out. He banged the flashlight against the palm of his hand. "Crap! I need new batteries."

"Go get 'em," Teddy demanded. "We haven't got all night."

"They're in the kitchen. Be right back." Ollie opened the door and tiptoed down the hallway. Gus trotted after him, thumping his tail against the wall. "Shhh!" The stairs creaked as someone descended. Ollie froze. A shadow moved across the landing. His heart pounded against his chest. "Who's there?"

"It's just me." DeeDee padded down the staircase in her bare feet. "What are you doing up so late?" She eyed him up and down. "And why are you dressed like a ninja?"

Ollie hid the flashlight behind his back. "Ninja? I don't know what you're talking about."

"Black clothes. Black bandana. Flashlight behind your back. Ya look like a ninja to me," she scoffed. "A ninja up to no good, I might add."

Busted. Ollie's shoulders drooped and his arms fell to his side, and the flashlight hit his thigh. His mind raced. He needed a reasonable explanation for his getup. DeeDee was a pest and a tattletale, but she wasn't stupid. Just then, Hank ripped down the stairs and slammed into the wall at the bottom of the steps. "Calm your stupid mutt," Ollie hissed. "He's gonna wake up Mom."

Too late. The creak of wooden floorboards sounded overhead. A sudden sliver of soft light shone from upstairs. Ollie panicked. Mom would be down any second—it was now or never. "Cover for me?"

"What?" DeeDee exclaimed, under her breath. "Why would I do that?"

"Because I need your help." He ducked out of sight behind the kitchen counter. Crouching, muscles tense, he kept his eyes locked on DeeDee. "Just this once, please."

"What am I supposed to do," she asked, gritting her teeth.

"You're an actress," he hissed. "Act!"

Mom came down the stairs and flipped the light switch. "Hey sweetie." She ruffled DeeDee's hair. "What are you doing up so late?"

DeeDee glanced sideways at Ollie. He held out his clasped hands to her in an imploring gesture. "Please," he mouthed.

"I, uh, just wanted to grab a glass of water." She made a little coughing sound. "Dry mouth," she added, tapping her throat.

Ollie watched Mom's reflection in the window, planning a quick scuttle around the counter if she made a move toward the kitchen.

"You okay?" Mom asked, feeling DeeDee's forehead with the back of her hand.

"Mom, stop fussing." She squirmed out of reach. "I'm just thirsty."

"I'll get you a glass of water." Mom said, taking a step forward.

"Nooo!" DeeDee cried. "I got it. Go back to bed. I'll be up in a minute."

"All right, already." Mom backed up, a wounded expression on her face. "But, don't dawdle, it's a school night." She scratched Gus behind the ears. "Why aren't you in Ollie's room, big guy?"

Ollie's hand flew over his mouth. Mom was about to take Gus back to his room. Unless DeeDee acted quickly, the jig was up.

"I got him." DeeDee rushed over and grabbed Gus by the collar. "I woke him up. I'll take him back."

"Thanks, sweetie." Mom turned and began to climb the stairs. Hank scampered underfoot. She knelt and gave the pug's smashed-in face a quick kiss. "Bedtime for you, too, Mr. Hanky." She pulled herself up to a stand and ascended the stairs. "Night-night."

DeeDee towered over Ollie, hands planted on her hips, head cocked to one side. "Whatever you're doing, this better not come back to bite me in the butt."

"It won't." Ollie grabbed hold of the kitchen counter and pulled himself up. "I just need a couple of hours."

A long minute passed in which nothing was heard but the *tick-tock* of the kitchen clock.

DeeDee closed her eyes and inhaled and slowly exhaled. She opened her eyes and began animatedly talking to herself. Her facial expression shifted from shock to outrage to concern. Ollie had seen this technique a million times. But why now?

"What are you doing?" he asked in an uneasy tone.

"I'm rehearsing my story for when you get caught." She scooped up Hank. "Now, it's time for me to go to bed. I need my beauty sleep." With a harrumph, she turned on her heel and marched upstairs.

———————————

A large cloud floated across the moon, giving the night a clandestine feeling. An owl swooped overhead and screeched while Ollie darted across the street, dashing from shadow to shadow.

"That was a close call with your mom." Teddy paraded down the middle of the road. "I thought for sure you were a goner."

"No kidding." Ollie peered out from behind a tree, shovel in hand. "DeeDee has never, ever covered for me. Weird."

"What's weird is you skulking about. Get a move on," Teddy urged. "Time's a-ticking!"

Ollie quickened his pace, abandoning the shadows for a full sprint down Peach Street. Car lights momentarily lit the road, and he ducked behind a trash can. A moment later, he continued on his way.

At the four-way stop, he took a shortcut through a back alley that dead-ended at the west side of Suds. He slowed to a walk, anxiety creeping through his body. The shovel weighed heavily in his grasp. A few minutes later, they arrived at the soccer field at back of the school.

Suds felt like a ghost town. It was so empty and quiet. A Doritos bag tumbled across the grassy field. Tetherball chains clanged against poles. The windows in the brick buildings gawked at him with dark, unblinking eyes.

A shiver ran down his spine. Too late to turn back now. He snaked along the border of the field, eyes darting. Scarcely daring to breathe, he skirted around the back of the multi-purpose room, finally rounding the corner to arrive at the oak tree. "Now what?"

Teddy circled the tree and took a gander around the quad. "If the house was over there . . ." He pointed toward Kelly Hall. "Then, I think you should dig here," he added, taking a step forward.

Ollie switched on the flashlight and hugged the wall, scanning the quad for unwelcome visitors. All clear. He aimed the light at the spot under the tree. The beam caught the outline of twisted roots and blades of grass. He pushed the shovel into the soil softened by the rain. The sound of metal hitting rock echoed in the quad. He froze. "Make sure we're alone."

"On it." Teddy disappeared. A minute later, he reappeared. "We're alone."

"Are you sure?"

"We're good. I promise."

Ollie started to dig in short bursts. Every few minutes, he stopped to pluck out debris that blocked his progress. Two hours later he stood in a hole the size of a kiddie pool. A pile of rocks lay at the foot of the tree. He stopped to wipe the sweat off his brow and glanced at his phone. "It's 2:45. We haven't got much time. How deep should I go?"

"Another foot and you should strike gold. That's *if* I'm a Kelly."

"I sure hope—" Ollie broke off as a police siren chirped to life and wailed. Panicking, he dove for cover in the hole and scrunched up into a tight little ball. The siren grew more and more distant until it faded away to nothing.

Teddy gazed down at him. "Whatcha doing?"

Ollie peered up from his foxhole. His face shone pale and anxious in the moonlight. "I thought for sure they were coming for me," he said, crawling to a stand. "Whatever!"

Teddy chuckled.

Grabbing the shovel, Ollie continued to dig. An hour later, the hole reached up to his waist. He thumbed on the flashlight and sifted through the dirt and rock. "I've got good news and bad news. The good news is I don't think you're a Kelly. The bad news—no gold."

CHAPTER 20
NEW HEADSTONE

Miss Sally dipped her brush into the can of paint and made broad strokes to cover the sign on her fence. "Even though I told you not to do something foolish, you went ahead and dug a hole on school grounds—in the middle of the night, no less."

"When was I supposed to do it?" Ollie objected. "Second period?"

She paused mid-stroke, drops of white paint dripping onto the gravel. Her mouth pulled down in a frown. "I understand how important it is for you to find the gold, but wandering around in the middle of the night is just plain dangerous."

"It's not like he was alone." Teddy snorted with indignation. "I was with him."

"Yes, that makes everything okay." Miss Sally continued to paint the fence.

"Anyway," Ollie interrupted. "I think it's safe to say Teddy is *not* a Kelly."

"Thank goodness." Teddy shuddered.

"Did you find the *Gazette* article?" Ollie asked, desperate for a new clue. "The one with Teddy's family in it."

"No." Miss Sally sighed heavily. "While you were out gallivanting last night, I was at the museum sifting through dusty newspaper archives. I couldn't find a thing, so it's back to the drawing board. You boys need to pick up where you left off. Do you still have the map I gave you?"

"It's in my bag." Ollie fished through his backpack and pulled out the map, smoothing it out on the sidewalk. "We already covered this area." He circled the map with his index finger. "I think we should focus on the streets closest to the river."

"We've only got two more days," Teddy reminded him. "We better get going."

"Let's start on Riverview Drive." Ollie shouldered his backpack and began hoofing it down the street. Glancing back, he called out to Miss Sally, "Wish us luck."

Miss Sally waved her paintbrush. "Good luck!"

"Let's cut through the park to save time," Teddy suggested. "Not sure why you had to sleep the morning away."

"Maybe it's because I was up until 4:00 in the morning." Ollie let out a big yawn. He was starting to feel his lack of sleep. His head felt like a bowling ball, and his limbs felt like noodles.

"You could've been home earlier."

"I told you," Ollie snapped. "Filling the hole back in was the right thing to do."

"What do you care? You're already doing the time. Why not do the crime?"

"Because contrary to popular belief, I'm not a jerk. Somebody could've fallen in and gotten hurt." He stopped at the corner of Riverview Drive and Fig Avenue. "Put a lid on it. We're here."

Historic homes sat perched on the bluff overlooking the river. Ancient oak trees shaded the winding lane. Referring to his map, Ollie traced his finger along a red street line. "Let's follow Riverview to Date Avenue, then crisscross our way back through the side alleys."

"I'll scout ahead. Meet me here." Teddy pointed to a small black cross on the map. "This shouldn't take too long."

"Got it. See ya in a few."

After a short hike, Ollie arrived at the rendezvous spot. A small stone church stood at the corner of Date Avenue and Spring Street. A wrought iron fence enclosed an old graveyard. Moldy, gray headstones poked out through tall weeds and creeping ivy.

"You know what they say about cemeteries?" Teddy appeared at the gate. "Hold your breath when you pass by. It will keep you safe from wandering spirits."

"Too late." Ollie smirked. "Any luck?"

"Nothing." Teddy sighed. "Sorry."

"I don't suppose you remember this place?" Ollie peered through the spiked metal fence at the creepy old cemetery.

"It's not a place I care to frequent." Teddy winced. "I don't like the headstones. They give me the heebie-jeebies." Walking through the fence, he wandered over to a stone slab with worn lettering and crumbling edges. "Take this one, for instance." He crouched down and read the grave marker aloud, "Tobias Smith, born April 24, 1834. Died January 1, 1861. Not a very Happy New Year if you ask me."

"Just think, you might have known some of these people," Ollie said, peering through the bars of the fence.

"That's not a very pleasant thought, how—"

"Holy cow!" Ollie exclaimed. "Your dad could be buried in here! Or maybe even . . ." His voice trailed off as he looked at Teddy.

"Ugh!" Teddy scrunched up his face and stuck his tongue out. "Don't even say it."

"Sorry." Ollie lifted the latch and opened the rusty gate. The hinges moaned in protest. Tall grass pushed back from the other side as if to block out the living. With a quick hip-check, he opened the gate, just enough to squeeze through. All was still. The air felt heavy and thick, and it was deathly quiet.

"This may take a while." Ollie aimed his finger at each tombstone, counting as he moved from crooked row to crooked row. "By my count, there are fifty-two." He glanced around to make sure they were alone. "I'll take the front half, you take the back."

"On it." Teddy moved to the rear of the cemetery until he reached the farthest gravestone, a large, gray slab, tilting precariously to one side. "Molly, wife of Jesse Cravens, died November 8, 1885. Age 54," he called out and moved on.

Ollie bent low and inspected a headstone covered in moss and white lichen. "Here lies the body of Benjamin Cartwright. Oh, crap!" He jerked backward, lost his balance and landed on his backside. "For a moment, I forgot there are actual bodies buried here." Scrambling to his feet, he stepped light-footed over a mound, making sure not to tread on a grave.

"I can't read the name on this one," Teddy grumbled, pressing his nose up to the tombstone.

"Move on to the next one. Unless our neighborhood tour jogs your memory, this may be our last shot at a clue."

The two boys went about their cryptic task with little conversation. An hour later, the sun shone high above the cemetery. Any hope of finding a new clue faded with the afternoon light. Ollie scraped away dead moss to reveal the name on the last marker: Mary Riley. His shoulders sagged. "Nothing. Nada. Zip."

"I know we need a clue . . . It's just, I'm relieved not to find one." Teddy twisted his shirt sleeve, shooting Ollie a sidelong glance. "I don't know how I'd feel about finding my final resting place."

"I'm sorry." Ollie arched his back and moved his neck from side to side to stretch his cramped muscles. "This must be really weird for you."

A white cat wandered into the cemetery, slinking through the tall, wet grass. It moved stealthily from headstone to headstone. Purring, it rubbed up against a small tombstone tucked away in a corner.

"Hey, kitty." Ollie reached out to scratch under the cat's chin. Instead of soft fur, his hand brushed up against the rough surface of the tombstone. "Eeew!" He pulled his hand back and shook it hard. "It's a ghost cat!"

"Oh, hey, Buttermilk," Teddy murmured, sinking down next to the feline. "How's my favorite kitty cat?"

"You have a cat?" Ollie took a step back. "Weird."

"What's wrong with that? You have a dog."

"True." Ollie eyed the fluffy white cat with renewed interest. "It's just you never mentioned your cat before."

"Never thought about it." Teddy shrugged. "I got her when I was five."

Buttermilk stretched languidly, pushed up to all fours, and stared with amber eyes at the shoebox-sized headstone, laying on the ground, broken in two.

"I missed this one." Ollie picked up both chunks and

inspected each side. "Looks like someone needs a new headstone."

Moving out of the shade and into the sunlight, he read the inscription on the larger portion. "Buttermilk . . . Beloved Cat." He turned and stared at Teddy. "Seriously? A burial site for your cat?"

"Back in my day, it wasn't uncommon for folks to bury their pets in the town graveyard." Teddy gestured to the fragment in Ollie's other hand. "What's written on the other piece?"

Ollie squinted at the lettering. "K-E, something, something. Family . . ." he drifted off without finishing the sentence. "Is that an N or an M after the E?" he asked, sticking the stone in Teddy's face.

"I think it's an M. Definitely. M."

"I think it's an N." Ollie placed the two sections carefully on the ground. "Definitely. N."

"I think you're wrong. It's an M."

"It's not. I'm pretty sure my eyesight is way better than yours. Most definitely, K-E-N."

"If you're sure . . ." Teddy's voice trailed off.

Ollie squinted at the lettering one more time. "I'm sure."

"Well, it may not be much, but at least we have two new letters." Teddy perked up. "So my last name begins with K-E-N. Ken. Ken. Ken. Ken," Teddy repeated over and over.

"Hmm. I got nothing." He shrugged. "But on the bright side, if Buttermilk was laid to rest here, we must be getting close."

Ollie stared at Teddy with his cat, curled up by his side. Things were definitely getting weird, but close? . . . He wasn't so sure about that.

CHAPTER 21
NEW NUGGET

"Kensington?" Ollie asked.

"No." Teddy shook his head.

"Kendell?"

"No."

"Kent?"

"No."

"Kennedy?"

Teddy regarded him thoughtfully. "Hmm . . . No."

"Argh!" Ollie threw his hands up in defeat. "I give up."

"You can't give up." Teddy strolled down Riverview Drive. "Every new clue brings us one step closer to finding the gold."

"School must be out." Ollie nodded toward a pair of kids on the bike trail. "I didn't realize it was so late." He pulled out his phone and checked the time. "Four-thirty? No wonder I'm so hungry."

The river sparkled in the afternoon sunlight. A flock of geese swooped down and landed on the shoreline, honking and flapping their wings. Above the racket, Ollie heard something far more obnoxious.

"Oi! Oxley!"

"Crap." Ollie watched in horror as Aubrey thumped across the bridge in their direction. "We don't have time for this." He spun around and retreated. Racing down the street, he swung a hard left and slid down an embankment, skinning his elbow along the way. At the bottom of the hill, he clambered to his feet and took off running. Adrenaline shot through his body, pushing him forward. Before long, he had a stitch in his side. Gasping for air, he scoured the terrain for a place to hide. The rugged trail sloped sharply downward. The stubby, brown grass lining the dirt path offered little to no cover.

"Over here." Teddy waved his arms. "She'll never look for you behind that bush."

Without stopping to ask why, Ollie left the path and tromped through the thick undergrowth that poked and scratched at his legs. After a quick check over his shoulder, he dove behind the clump of bushes and flattened his body against the ground.

Aubrey charged down the trail in hot pursuit. Little puffs of dust exploded around her feet with each step. Pulling to a stop, she doubled over to catch her breath a few yards from Ollie's hiding spot. "I bloody well know you're here somewhere, Oxley," she gasped, hands on her knees, gazing around.

Birds chirped in response.

Ollie peered through the bright red and green leaves of

the clumpy bush, his muscles tense, ready to spring into action. A bead of sweat trickled down the side of his face, tickling him. He twitched his mouth to satisfy the itch.

Aubrey made a final sweep of the area, then continued down the trail. At the bottom of the hill, she swerved right and disappeared. Ollie exhaled a deep sigh of relief and rolled onto his back. Teddy stood over him, hands planted on his hips.

Ollie gave him a grateful smile. "Thanks, dude. How did ya know she wouldn't look here?"

"Only a fool would hide behind a poison oak bush." Teddy chuckled.

"What the—" Ollie jumped to his feet and backed away, eyeing the offensive foliage. "Not cool, dude. Not cool."

"You're welcome." Teddy squinted his eyes with sarcasm. "That's the thanks I get for saving your hide?"

"You didn't save my hide. I'm just not in the mood to deal with Aubrey." Ollie's stomach suddenly rumbled. "I'm tired and hungry. I'm going home."

"We can't stop now. We still have a lot more ground to cover."

"You're not stopping. I am." Ollie turned and hiked back up the hill. "I'm not a ghost. I need food."

"Fine. You've got twenty minutes. Then I'm coming to get you."

———————

Ollie inhaled a ham sandwich and took a swig of milk. Exhausted, he stretched out on the floor beside his bed. *Just a short nap . . .*

"You eat like a pig," Teddy scolded. "Wipe your mouth. You have crumbs all over your face. Also, take a bath, Just because we're running out of time doesn't mean you should abandon all hygiene."

Ollie's eyes fluttered open and stretched wide. Teddy sat perched on the bed, and his dirty feet dangled over the edge, inches from Ollie's face. "You're one to talk. When was the last time you took a bath?" he grumbled, eyeballing Teddy's filthy feet. "By the way, what happened to your big toe? No Band-Aids in the 1800s?"

"That's an excellent question." Teddy flexed his legs and examined his toe. "If I remember right, I stubbed it on a stepping-stone when I was running to the outhouse. That's when I fell and knocked my noggin."

"Outhouse? You had to go to the bathroom outside? Yuck. No wonder your feet are so dirty," Ollie said, with a new appreciation for indoor plumbing. "Wait a minute . . ." He bolted upright and gaped at Teddy. "Did you say stepping-stones?"

"Yes," Teddy answered, with a questioning gaze. "The stepping-stones went all the way from our back door to the outhouse."

Ollie tried to organize his racing thoughts. A picture was beginning to form in his mind like the pieces of a puzzle snapping into place. He needed one final clue to solve the mystery. "What did you say your dad buried the gold in?" he asked, feeling a rush of excitement.

"I didn't. But I think a wooden chest. Why?"

"Be more specific!" Ollie shouted. "Think!"

"All right. All right. Take it easy." Teddy tilted his head back and stroked his chin. "If I remember correctly, it was a wooden chest bound by iron bands with a lock."

"I can't believe we didn't see this before." Ollie shook his head in disbelief. "It's been right under our noses the whole time."

"What's been under our noses?"

"Follow me!" He scrambled to his feet and raced out the door.

"But I don't follow you!"

"No, follow me!" Ollie ran down the hall with Gus barking and nipping at his heels. At the back of the house, he reached for the doorknob. Teddy shot past him and straight through the wall.

"Show-off," Ollie muttered and followed him outside. In the backyard, he hurried over to the oak tree and knelt down to examine the piece of metal poking out from the trunk.

"That's fascinating," remarked Teddy. "Still not sure what you're freaking out about."

"Don't you see?" Ollie exclaimed. "*This* was your house!"

"I can assure you, I did not live in a *pink* house. I think I'd know if this was my house."

"Look at the stepping-stones. Look where they go." Ollie made a grand gesture at the small building at the back of the yard.

"Yes, I see." Teddy shrugged his shoulders. "So?"

"Dude! Get a clue. Under all that ivy is your outhouse."

"Jumpin' catfish!" Teddy skipped across the stepping-stones. "One, two, three, four, five, six—lucky number seven." He spun around to face Ollie. "This is my house! You're a genius."

"Yes, I am. This piece of metal must be what's left of the chest," Ollie explained, running his hand over the metal band. "I knew it was something important the first time I saw it."

"Well, what are you waiting for? Go fetch a shovel."

"On my way!" Ollie's feet barely touched the ground as he raced to the front yard. He grabbed the shovel from under the porch, swung it over his shoulder, and ran back. "Where should I dig?"

Teddy circled the tree, walked through the tree, and then reappeared sitting on a branch of the tree. From his perch, he aimed his stubbed toe at a spot to the right of the tree. "There. Dig there. My pa buried it on this side of the tree, facing the house."

Ollie gripped the shovel and jabbed it into the ground.

The blade crunched and cut through the packed dirt and thick roots.

After an hour of heavy labor, he set aside the shovel and worked the soil with his hands. Mounds of dirt lay scattered around the yard. He wiped the dirt and perspiration from his forehead and rocked back on his heels.

Teddy hung upside down by his knees from a tree branch, swinging back and forth like a trapeze artist. "You look like you just lost a mud-pie-eating contest."

Ollie plopped down onto a pile of dirt. "Gee, thanks. As usual, you're about as helpful as—"

"Crackers and crawfish!" Teddy disappeared. A split second later, he reappeared next to the large hole.

"Really?" Ollie scowled. "You couldn't just walk over? Your disappearing act is kind of annoying."

"I may be annoying, but I am useful." Teddy pointed at a glint of gold sparkling in the sunlight.

"I see it!" Ollie's eyes lit up. Crawling on his hands and knees, he scooped up the ball of hard dirt and rock. With trembling hands, he broke apart the earth and dislodged a gold nugget the size of a golf ball. "Whoa! Look at the size of this rock."

"That's nothing. Keep digging. You're about to hit the mother lode."

Ollie shoved the gold nugget in his front pocket and clambered to his feet. Grabbing hold of the shovel, he planted his foot on the blade and stomped it into the ground. He continued to dig until he found another gold nugget and then another and then another. It felt like Christmas morning, only way better. Every precious new nugget made him giddy with joy.

CHAPTER 22
NEW BUCKET

Ollie sifted through the dirt with a trowel, separating the rock from the soil. Coils of green rubber hose snaked through the grass, around the tree, to the edge of the hole. Water flowed freely from the nozzle. He dropped a pile of rocks into the gold pan, added water, then swirled the mixture in circles until the hard dirt melted away. Holding a nugget up, he examined it in the sunlight. "Hello, my friend," he said, planting a kiss on the gold before tossing it into a bucket. "I wonder how much it's worth?"

"Uh-oh." Teddy lifted his chin toward the house. "Your family's home."

Ollie's gaze shifted to the house. His mom and sister peered through the window in the door. DeeDee pressed her nose up against the glass, gaping at him. Mom's face turned bright red. He glanced down at his mud-spattered clothes, suddenly realizing what a mess he'd made. The backyard looked like a gopher convention had just blown through town. Piles of dirt and rock lay scattered about the yard and Gus was rolling around in the mud.

"You've got some explaining to do." Teddy chuckled. "You

better talk fast, because it looks like you're about to get a whooping."

"Hey, Mom." Ollie waved for her to come outside.

Mom disappeared from the window. Seconds later, she exited the house and picked her way around the fresh mounds of dirt. DeeDee followed close behind.

Hank raced outside and lapped up water from a murky puddle.

"I came home to say I'm sorry for not sticking up for you at school. I know you would never trash the school garden." Mom's gaze swept over the disaster scene. "But after seeing this mess, I'm not so sure. What on earth has gotten into you?"

"I think it's a cry for help," DeeDee said, pretending to be all grown up. "I saw something like this in a movie. Troubled kids often act out to get attention."

"Zip it, *Delilah*," Ollie snapped, wiping a smudge of dirt from his cheek.

DeeDee stuck out her tongue in reply.

"I found a buried stash of gold," Ollie said, his eyes fixed on Mom.

"I think you've been out in the sun too long. Let's get you inside, get you cooled off, and cleaned up." Mom felt his forehead with the back of her hand. "Then we can talk about what's going on with you."

"I'm not kidding. Captain Cook is rich." He nudged a

bucket with his foot; gold nuggets tumbled to the ground. "He can pay the bank, so we don't have to move."

Mom flashed him an irritated look but moved slightly forward. She bent down to study the rocks. "What is all this?" She held a gold nugget up to the sunlight, turning it from side to side. The corners of her mouth twitched toward an uncertain smile. "Oh, my goodness . . ." her voice trailed off. She gazed up at Ollie. "This is gold. This really is gold." Her voice grew louder with excitement. "THIS REALLY, REALLY IS GOLD!" Standing up, she threw her arms around Ollie, hugging him so tight he let loose a tiny squeak. "Oops, I'm sorry." She giggled, releasing him.

"Watch out for the gold pan," Ollie warned. Too late. Mom stumbled and fell to the ground, laughing.

"Oh my, I'm literally tripping over gold," she said, ogling the treasure.

DeeDee leapt over a pile of rocks, splashed though a mud puddle, crashed head-on into Ollie, and gave him a bear hug. "This is just like a scene from a movie!" she exclaimed. "Hero swoops in at the last minute and saves the day! And, because he's so brave and kind he uses the gold to pay for his sister's voice and dance lessons. I need to be a triple threat if I'm going to make it in show biz," she added, flashing jazz hands.

"It's Captain Cooks' backyard, so you better ask him." Ollie chuckled. "But maybe he'll give me a finder's fee."

"But what made you dig here in the first place?" Mom asked.

Ollie glanced sideways at the metal poking out from the trunk of the tree. "Uh . . . I saw this weird piece of metal and thought there might be something important buried here."

"Well, lucky for us you were right. I need to call Captain Cook. He's never going to believe this." Mom reached into her pocket and pulled out her cell phone. After punching in the number, she got up and paced around the yard as she spoke, "Cookie, have I got news for you."

"Speaking of good news . . . I should call on Miss Sally." Teddy beamed. "I'll ask her to bring the metal detector."

"Metal detector?"

"What are you mumbling about?" DeeDee asked.

"You know . . . a device that detects metal," Teddy said, shaking his head. "Duh!"

"Yes, a metal detector would be most helpful," Ollie grumbled. "That would have been nice to have *before* digging a hole at Suds."

DeeDee shot a wary glance around the yard and then looked back at Ollie. "Who are you talking to?"

"Uh-oh." Teddy chuckled and disappeared.

———————

"Welcome to the gold rush!" Ollie greeted Captain Cook and Miss Sally when they arrived in the backyard. "Did you bring the metal detector?"

"Sure did." Miss Sally held up a contraption that resembled a golf club with a small steering wheel attached to the end. "How much have you got so far?"

"Buckets full." Ollie stepped aside so they could see the gold. "Teddy never said there'd be this much."

"You never asked." Teddy hooked his thumbs on his suspenders and leaned against the oak tree.

"Teddy?" Captain Cook gazed around at all the happy faces. "Who's Teddy?"

"Yeah." DeeDee scooted up next to Ollie and gave him a playful hip bump. "Who is this Teddy?"

"Uhhh." Ollie glanced at Miss Sally for assistance.

"Teddy is a docent at the museum," Miss Sally jumped in to help. "He told Ollie quite a story about a gold prospector who buried his gold for safekeeping."

"Aye." Captain Cook rubbed the dark stubble on his chin. "Why don't you show me this treasure before we all get too carried away?"

"See for yourself. You're rich!" Ollie gestured toward the gold pan, a bucket, and Mom's favorite spaghetti pot. All three containers were overflowing with gold nuggets. He reached down to grab the bucket, but it was so heavy the handle broke. "Whoa! I guess we need a new bucket."

Captain Cook eyes widened and his mouth dropped open like a Pez dispenser. Falling to one knee, he snatched the largest nugget from the spaghetti pot. "Shiver me timbers.

This is gold." Climbing to his feet, he wiped his misty eyes and placed his large hands on Ollie's shoulders. "Do you know what this means, lad?" His eyes crinkled at the corners as his mouth spread into a wide grin. "You saved the Bing and Cook's!"

"If you say so," Ollie said with a gleam in his eye.

"I wonder whose gold it was," Mom said. "This is quite a fortune for someone to have left behind."

"Yes, I wonder." Miss Sally scrutinized the metal band. She patted down her pockets, searching for something. "Ollie, I don't have my glasses. Are those letters?"

"Yup." Ollie locked eyes with Miss Sally. "All I could make out was *W-A-L*."

"That's W-A-L-T-E-R, as in 'Walter' for my pa." Teddy beamed with pride.

"Now he remembers," Ollie said under his breath and chuckled softly.

CHAPTER 23
NEW PRESIDENT

The next morning, the jangle of the home phone woke Ollie from a nightmare. In his dream, Aubrey had stolen the gold and used it to buy votes and win the election. Yawning, he rubbed his sleep-crusted eyes and stretched his arms wide.

Mom poked her head inside the door. "It's Mr. Ritter." She covered the receiver with her hand. "Is there something you need to tell me?" she asked, giving him the fish-eye.

"Uh . . ." Alarm bells went off inside his head. He sat up stick-straight. Fear crept through his body like a slow-moving wildfire. An endless list of worst-case scenarios tumbled around inside his head. First and foremost, his midnight excursion to Suds. *Busted!*

"Not that I can think of," he answered in his best I've-got-no-idea-what-you're-talking-about voice. Warily, he took the phone from his mom and cradled it to his ear. "Hello?"

"Good morning, Oliver." The matter-of-fact tone of Mr. Ritter's voice offered little indication of his mood or the purpose of his call. "I'd like to see you in my office first thing this morning."

"This morning?" Ollie gripped the cold plastic receiver. "Y-y-your office?"

"Yes. My office," he replied. "There are things we need to discuss."

"Discuss?" Ollie tugged at what was left of his eyebrow. "I-I-I guess I could be there in about half an hour."

"Good. I'll be waiting." There was a click and the line went dead. For a brief moment, Ollie listened to the dull sound of the dial tone. This could only mean one thing—more trouble.

"Well?" Mom stared at him expectantly. "What'd he say?"

"He wants me at school." Ollie raked his fingers through his tangled hair and slowly sank back onto the bed. Mom sat down next to him and put a hand on his knee. "Do you want me to go? I have to work, but I can cancel rehearsals."

"No." He flashed his best reassuring smile. "I'll be okay. I can handle whatever he has to say."

Thirty minutes later, Ollie parked his bike and trudged toward the office. There wasn't a kid in sight. Everyone was in class, except for him. His stomach did flip-flops. Breathing deeply to calm his nerves, he wiped his sweaty palms on his shorts and reached for the handle.

Just then the door flew open with a loud *bang*. Cinda and Sierra pushed past him in a flurry of tears. Ollie scrambled to get out of their way. "Nice to see you, too," he mumbled sarcastically, waving at them as they hurried away.

Two sets of parents exited the office. All four wore serious expressions. *Me thinks the gargoyles are in trouble.* He moved aside to let them pass, then turned back to face the door. His pulse quickened. Bracing for the worst, he opened the door, stepped inside, and prepared to meet his fate.

Ollie waited for a few seconds as the secretary tapped away at her computer. He dug his fingernails into the palm of his hand to calm his nerves. Finally he cleared his throat and said, "I'm here to see Mr. Ritter. My mom had to work, so it's just me, Ollie Oxley."

The secretary peeled her gaze away from the computer screen, her fingers hovering above the keyboard. Dipping her head, she studied him over the rim of her glasses. "Mr. Ritter is expecting you. Go right in."

"Thank you"—Ollie glanced down at the name plaque perched on the edge of her desk—"Miss Vicky."

"You're welcome." A quick smile flickered across her face as she turned her attention back to the computer screen. With a quick flip of her hand, she dismissed him and said, "Move along. He doesn't like to be kept waiting."

Ollie stood rooted to the ground. In his experience, visits to the principal's office only meant one thing—trouble. Why should today be any different? His legs felt like lead as he headed towards Mr. Ritter's office. What he needed right now was a good excuse for his midnight excursion. *Sleepwalking?*

A cry for help? A ghost made me do it? The door was ajar. He knocked lightly. It swung open.

Mr. Ritter glanced up from his desk. "Good morning, son," he said motioning for him to take a seat. "Sit."

Son? Ollie lowered himself onto the chair and flicked a tongue over his dry lips. His T-shirt stuck to his back like Saran Wrap. He crossed and uncrossed his feet and gripped the sides of the chair.

"It appears I owe you an apology, young man," Mr. Ritter confessed. "It turns out that you were, indeed, set up by Aubrey Kelly. Upon further questioning, Sierra and Cinda admitted to lying about your involvement."

Teddy sprang up from behind Mr. Ritter's chair like a crazed jack-in-the-box and exclaimed, "When confronted with the truth, Boo and Hoo fessed up like a couple of rat-faced turncoats. I don't think we'll be seeing them anytime soon."

Ollie maintained eye contact with Mr. Ritter. His heartbeat quickened as the words sank in. He fought the urge to gawp at Teddy. "I knew it," he muttered to himself.

"They're outta here!" Teddy hooked his thumb in the air and shouted like a baseball umpire. "Hasta la pasta. Adiós, muchachos."

"Knock it off," Ollie blurted out.

"Excuse me?" Mr. Ritter raised a curious eyebrow. "Knock what off?"

"What I meant to say is that they need to knock it off," Ollie replied, sounding foolish, even to himself. "You know, the lying."

"Yes, they do," Mr. Ritter agreed. "Apparently, Gurdeep saw the whole thing. Aubrey destroyed the garden, then persuaded her friends to lie."

Ollie frowned. "I'm glad Gurdeep came forward, but what took so long?"

Mr. Ritter rubbed the side of his face as he formulated his answer. "That's a question for Gurdeep. But let's just say he's been dealing with Aubrey a lot longer than you have."

Ollie nodded in sudden understanding. For years he had moved from town to town, school to school, bully to bully. Whenever the going got tough, a new move would provide a welcome escape. Gurdeep was stuck in the same town, going to the same school, dealing with the same bully. Maybe his role as the perpetual new kid had its advantages.

"So what do you think?" Mr. Ritter asked, clearly waiting for an answer.

"Think?" Ollie shook his head clear and looked around bewildered

"Yes. Between the schoolwork you missed and your duties as class president, you have a lot to catch up on."

"Class president?" Ollie exclaimed. "Are you kidding?"

"No." Mr. Ritter finally cracked a smile. "You won by a landslide."

"Awesome." Ollie heaved a sigh of relief and relaxed into the chair. His fingers tingled as he unclenched his fists.

"See!" Teddy exclaimed. "Now, that is *awesome*!"

Mr. Ritter pulled a hall pass out of the desk drawer, and began to write. "This should keep the hall monitor at bay. He can be a little overzealous at times."

"Tell me about it." Ollie frowned at the memory of the day he got suspended.

"Now it's time for you to get to class. I'm sure your friends would like to say hello to their new president. Oh, before you go . . ." Mr. Ritter opened a side drawer in his desk and pulled out a green, leather-bound book with gold letters embossed across the cover: *Sudbury Middle School, Class President Handbook*. "This is for you," he said, handing Ollie the book with the hall pass. "Get yourself up to speed."

"Yes, sir." Ollie rose to his feet and reached out to grab the manual. It felt heavier than it looked. "Thank you." He cracked it open and shuffled out of the office with his face in the book. On his way out, he bumped into Miss Vicky's desk. Pens rattled in the coffee cup she used as a pencil holder. Her eyebrows shot up, and she smiled broadly. "Congratulations, Mr. Oxley. It seems like you're on a winning streak."

Ollie clutched the book tightly to his chest, afraid that if he let go, all of his newfound happiness might slip away. "I guess I am." He smiled and turned toward Teddy. "Thanks to my best friend." Reaching for the door, he pulled it open and stepped out into the deserted hall.

"What would you do without me?" Teddy skipped alongside him. "First the gold, now this. I am the best partner a guy could ever have."

"My partner the ghost." Ollie reflected on their unlikely friendship. "Weirder things have happened. I just can't think of any."

The P.A. system crackled to life. The corridor filled with the sound of static, followed by a six-bell chime. "Attention everyone," said Miss Vicky. "Mr. Ritter would like to make an important announcement."

Mr. Ritter cleared his throat and spoke, "Attention, students. I'm happy to announce that your new seventh-grade class president is . . . Ollie Oxley!"

Wild cheers and applause erupted in the classrooms and echoed down the hallway.

Mr. Ritter continued, "Please welcome Ollie back and congratulate him on his win."

"You can thank your campaign manager for that." Teddy jerked a thumb at his chest. "Ghosts rule! Bullies drool!"

Ollie opened the door to homeroom. A chorus of cheers greeted him when he walked into the room. Aubrey and the gargoyles were noticeably absent. He assumed they must have been suspended, or even better, expelled.

"Welcome back, Mr. Oxley," Mr. Miller greeted him with

a huge smile. "I'm sorry I jumped to conclusions," he apologized, clapping Ollie warmly on the back. "Please accept my most sincere apology."

"Sure thing, Mr. Miller." Ollie glanced around the room at all the smiling faces. All, that is, except for one. Gurdeep slumped down in his chair and lowered his head. Ollie crossed the room and tapped him on the shoulder. "Thanks, dude."

"You're not mad?" Gurdeep asked, sitting up straight. "I was gonna warn you, but then you said you were moving, and, well . . . I chickened out. I didn't want to deal with Aubrey. I blew it. I'm sorry."

"We're cool." Ollie swiped his hand though the air. "You came through in the end and that's all that matters."

"It wasn't just because you found the gold," Gurdeep quickly added. "I went in first thing this morning, before I knew."

"Speaking of the gold," Mr. Miller interrupted. "I think we'd all love to hear how you came to discover this long-lost treasure."

With all eyes on him, Ollie told the story he and Teddy had concocted. "The first time I saw this strange piece of metal poking out from a tree in my backyard, I knew it was important," Ollie began. "So when Mr. Ritter gave me a little *time off*," he said, making air quotes, "I decided to investigate."

"Nice of Bitter Ritter to give you a vacation," Mikayla teased. "Maybe after school, we can grab an ice cream at Cook's."

"Uh. Yeah." Ollie's face lit up. "Captain Cook did offer me free ice cream for life. I'm sure he wouldn't mind if I brought you along."

Teddy rolled his eyes and made gagging noises, which, of course, Ollie ignored.

CHAPTER 24

NEW INFORMATION

"I'll get it!" Ollie ran his fingers through his hair and tucked his T-shirt into his shorts. Hank and Gus sprinted toward the front door like the house was on fire. "Just a second," Ollie yelled over the commotion. After calming the dogs down, he opened the door. "Hey, guys, you're early," he greeted Miss Sally and Captain Cook. "The photographer from the *Granite City Gazette* won't be here for another thirty minutes. How do you like my new shirt?" he asked, pulling his T-shirt taut to fully display the Gold Country logo of a forty-niner hunched over, panning for gold. "It'll look good on camera, don't ya think?"

"It's perfect," Miss Sally said, giving him a quick hug. "We came early because we need to talk."

"It's important." Captain Cook's eyes twinkled, and his mustache twitched ever so slightly. "Let your mom and DeeDee know we're here."

"Is something wrong?" Ollie felt a lump in his throat

the size of a jawbreaker. "Was there not enough gold to pay the bank?"

"Let's just get everyone together," Miss Sally answered with a mysterious smile.

Ollie followed them down the hall to the living room. He could hear Mom singing along to the radio in the kitchen. The smell of chocolate chip pancakes still hung in the air from breakfast.

"We've got company," Ollie shouted, giving Miss Sally a sideways glance.

The visitors sat down on the couch and waited for everyone to gather. Ollie lowered himself to the floor and sat cross-legged, never taking his eyes off Miss Sally. She was wearing an unreadable expression on her face. Gus stretched out beside him, and Hank curled up into a little ball at his feet.

DeeDee raced down the stairs two steps at a time and screeched to a stop in front of the hall mirror. Tilting her head at different angles, she brushed her bangs out of her eyes and blew herself a kiss. "What's up?" she asked, dropping down on the floor next to Ollie.

Ollie shrugged his shoulders but offered no response, fearful his voice might crack. His mouth was dry and pasty and his body buzzed with adrenaline.

"Hey, guys." Mom walked into the room, wiping her hands on a checkered dishtowel. "You're early. Is everything okay?"

She tucked a wisp of hair behind her ear and stared point-edly at Miss Sally and Captain Cook. "You look so serious."

"Maybe you should take a seat." Captain Cook stood up and gestured to a chair. "We have new information."

Mom settled into her favorite plaid armchair, folded the dishtowel in half, and laid it across her lap. She glanced over at Ollie and DeeDee and gave them a quick wink and a reassuring smile.

Miss Sally gazed around the room to make sure she had everyone's undivided attention. Satisfied that all eyes were on her, she spoke, "The letters *W-A-L* engraved in the metal got me thinking, so I went to the county recorder's office to do a little research." She paused for a moment to let her words sink in. Captain Cook nodded for her to continue. "I pulled the records for this house and made a startling discovery."

Ollie suspected this story did not have a happy ending. "What kind of records?" he asked, feeling like his brain was about to short-circuit.

"The kind of records that show who originally owned this property." Miss Sally gave him a meaningful stare. "The kind of discovery that changes people's lives."

"I believe any living family members of the prospec-tor who buried the gold have a rightful claim to the gold," Captain Cook said. "I won't be hornswoggling anyone out of their treasure."

"Well, of course, that makes sense. Why didn't we think

of that?" Mom fiddled with the dishtowel and shifted in her chair. "Oh, Cookie, I'm so sorry. Have you been able to find anyone?"

"Aye." Captain Cook nodded. "They live right here in Granite City."

"Walter E. Kemp was the original owner." Miss Sally leaned forward and placed a hand on Mom's knee.

"Kemp?" Mom looked as if she had just swallowed a fly.

"Aye, Jenny . . . Kemp." Captain Cook grinned, his gold tooth sparkling.

"There's more," Miss Sally continued, turning to face Ollie. "Walter and his wife, Marjorie, had two sons, Theodore and Elias. Walter was a gold miner who struck it rich during the Gold Rush. Unfortunately, he didn't live long enough to enjoy his newfound wealth. He died a short time later, taking with him the secret of where he buried the gold. His son, Theodore, followed him in death soon after. This left Marjorie and Elias alone and penniless."

"The 1800s were hard times," Captain Cook added with a sad shake of his head. "That was when my great-great-grandfather bought this house. It's been in my family ever since."

"Hey, Mom, isn't Kemp your maiden name?" Ollie asked. This new information felt like a technology overload. His systems were about to crash.

"Yes, dear," Mom replied, white as a ghost.

"But then that would mean . . ." Ollie couldn't finish the sentence.

"We're related!" Teddy completed the sentence for him. "I told you it was an *M* and not an *N* on the headstone. We could have saved ourselves a bunch of time if you had just listened to me."

"What?" Ollie spun around to face Teddy.

"Turns out, I'm your great-great-great-uncle." Teddy's grin stretched from ear to ear. "You can call me Uncle Teddy."

"I am not calling you Uncle Teddy," Ollie whispered, out the side of his mouth. "Not happening."

DeeDee scoured the room for a new arrival. "Who's Uncle Teddy?"

"Just my imaginary friend." Ollie rolled his eyes and chuckled. "Thankfully, there's only one Teddy. I don't think I could handle ten of him."

Mom just stared at Captain Cook. "So . . . what are you saying?" Mom asked.

"I'm saying the gold is rightfully yours," said Captain Cook. "I'm not the rich one in town. You, my dear friends, are."

CHAPTER 25
NEW ATTITUDE

"Let's try this one more time." Mom flipped through the pages of the script. "Start at the beginning of Act Two."

"Again?" whined the actor playing Velma. "I'm tired, and my feet are killing me."

"Yeah, well, your timing is killing me." Mom sighed. "Again, please."

A collective groan arose among the cast members. A backup dancer flopped to the floor and lay back with his hands over his face. "Not again!"

Mom held up both hands to quiet everybody down. "Enough already. Take a five-minute break. And please come back with a new attitude." She whispered into Ollie's ear, "Actors! They're such drama queens."

"No kidding," Ollie agreed. "But don't let DeeDee hear you say that."

"Mum's the word." Mom smiled. "You know, if I didn't know better, I might think you were enjoying the show."

"I guess I am." Ollie gazed around the old theater. He settled back into the chair and felt the plush cushion beneath his palm. The smell of fresh paint tickled his nose.

Red velvet curtains framed the stage. He tapped his fingers to the beat of the jazz music playing over the sound system.

"I'm glad to see you so happy," Mom said. "I like your new attitude."

"It's weird. I've never liked the theater, but now, it kinda feels like home."

"That's because it's not going anywhere." Mom put her arm around his shoulder. "And neither are we." She reached into her bag and pulled out a bulky manila envelope. "Would you mind running this next door?"

"Sure, Mom. Break a leg." He kissed her on the cheek, got up from his comfy chair, and ducked out of the dark theater. Outside, it took a moment to adjust to the bright sunlight. He shielded his eyes against the glare with the manila envelope. A cloud drifted across the sky, blocking the sun and chilling the air. "Excuse me," he said, after bumping into someone on the sidewalk.

"No problem," said a familiar voice. "It's my fault. I didn't see you coming."

Ollie lowered the envelope and frowned. "Oh. Hey, Aubrey." There was something different about her, but he couldn't quite put his finger on it. *Wait a minute . . . What happened to her accent?*

"I owe you an apology," she mumbled.

"Ya think?" Ollie scoffed. "You got me suspended!"

Aubrey bit her lip. A sudden change came over her face.

Her expression softened and her face flushed. She brushed the hair out of her eyes and blinked furiously. "I'm sorry. I've been a complete jerk. My mom has this weird thing about winning and, well . . ." Her eyes welled up and clear snot dripped down onto her lip. "To be honest, it's exhausting."

"Aww, jeez." Ollie patted her on the shoulder in an awkward gesture. "Don't cry. I forgive you."

Aubrey wiped the snot from her nose with the back of her hand. "Really?

"Yeah, I guess." He wrinkled his nose in disgust. "Just don't ask me to shake your hand."

"Deal," she cried, extending her snot-covered hand.

Without thinking, Ollie stuck his hand out to shake hers. "Deal."

Aubrey yanked her hand back just in time and laughed. "You almost got my snot cooties."

It took Ollie a moment to realize that Aubrey was not laughing at him, but with him.

"That was close." He smiled. *Maybe she's not so bad after all.*

"By the way, I heard about the gold. What are you gonna do with all the money?"

"Well, let's just say I'm not going anywhere anytime soon." Ollie clutched the manila envelope in his hand. "We just bought ourselves a pink house. So, I guess you'd better get used to seeing me around. Speaking of going somewhere, I heard your mom is sending you to live on a pig farm."

"Ferret farm," she corrected. "I'm going to live with my Aunt Ruby. She owns a ferret farm in New Mexico. My mom says I need a new attitude."

"Don't feel bad. I've had a bit of an attitude adjustment myself. Are you ever coming back?"

"Yeah, I'll be back next summer. In the meantime—"

BAM!

The door to Cook's Candy flew open. Mrs. Kelly stormed outside, ripped a stack of papers in half and threw them into the air. They scattered in the wind. She turned and locked eyes with Ollie, her face contorted with rage. "Thanks a lot for sharing your gold with Cook. You just cost me a building."

Ollie said nothing in reply.

Mrs. Kelly pushed past him and grabbed Aubrey roughly by the arm. "Come on. You have a plane to catch."

A sudden change came over Aubrey's face. Her expression turned hard and her eyes narrowed. "Later, loser."

And she's back, Ollie thought. But this time, he didn't hold it against her. She had enough problems to deal with.

CHAPTER 26
NEW HOME

Ollie kicked back in the shade of the oak tree with Gus by his side. Newly grown grass covered the spot where he and Teddy had discovered their gold. Red snapdragons and yellow marigolds bloomed in the flower bed. A squirrel scampered along the new redwood fence, and Gus sprang into action.

"The talent show starts in ten minutes," DeeDee shouted from the upstairs window. "If you want a good seat, you'd better get out to the front yard. Miss Sally and Captain Cook are already front row and center."

"Whatever, drama queen," Ollie yelled. "I'll take my chances." He glanced over his shoulder at the bent piece of metal in the oak tree. So much had changed in the last few months. Teddy had found his old home, and now Ollie had a new home. His new house was his family's old house and his new friend was an old ghost—who just happened to be his great-great-great-uncle. It was a new beginning for his family and he couldn't be happier.

"Hey sweetie." Mom got up from the rattan chaise lounge and walked over to Ollie. Fanning out a handful of cards in different shades of blue and green, she asked, "What color do you like best?"

"Blue, of course," Ollie said. "What's it for?"

"I thought, now that we own the house, we could have it painted this summer."

Ollie jerked upright and shook his head. "No. No way."

"I thought you hated pink," Mom said, with a bemused smile.

"I do. I mean, I did. It's just, pink kinda makes me feel happy. Weird. Huh?"

"Well, all righty then, our new home stays pink." Mom stuffed the cards into her back pocket. "I'll see you out front."

Buttermilk padded across the lawn and rubbed up against the oak tree. She sat down and curled her tail across her paws.

Plink!

An acorn landed on Ollie's head.

Plink! Plink! Plink!

"Teddy!"

Plink! Plink! Plink!

"I refuse to call you Uncle Teddy. You can flick acorns at me all day long, and I'll still never, ever call you Uncle Teddy."

"But we both know I'm older and wiser," Teddy declared from his perch in the tree.

"Older, yes. Wiser, now that's debatable."

"I don't know about that." Teddy kicked his legs back

and forth. "If it weren't for me, your mom could never have bought this house. And you, my dear nephew, might have ended up in Timbuktu."

"I hear Timbuktu is beautiful this time of year."

"Jumpin' catfish. You're a stubborn cuss."

"I wonder what side of the family I get that from."

"Certainly not mine. I'm as easygoing as a pig in a puddle."

"Whatever, dude."

"I'd like to say my work is done." Teddy dropped another acorn on Ollie's head. "But I have a feeling my job has just begun."

"Yes, I'm such a mess. Not sure how I've made it this far without you."

"Glad to see we agree." Teddy jumped down from the tree. "So, are you ready for our next adventure? I hear a search is on for the old Granite City mine. I may know someone who can help."

"Please tell me it's *not* the spirit of a second cousin or something." Ollie smiled. "One ghost in the family is about all I can take."

"Well . . ." Teddy hooked his thumbs on his suspenders and flashed his dimples. "I can't make any promises."

ACKNOWLEDGMENTS

Writing a book is a daunting task, nearly impossible if you venture forth on your own. But as luck would have it, the universe saw to it that I would not have to walk this path alone.

First and foremost, I want to thank my editor, Carlisa Cramer. The girl who made my dream come true. I will never forget the moment I received your email offering me a book deal. It was one of the most joyful moments of my life. Your kindness and generosity guided me through acquisitions, edits, and the entire publishing process. Thank you for pushing me to dig deeper with each round of edits. You are brilliant!

A huge thank you to everyone at Jolly Fish Press. Seriously, I am a bubbling fountain of gratitude. What an incredible team! To my managing editor, Mari Kesselring, thank you for believing in my little ghost story. Thank you, Sarah Taplin, for my fantastic book cover and interior design. And thank you, Megan Naidl, for your stellar marketing and publicity campaign.

Nobody picks up a book unless they love the cover. Thank you to my illustrator, George Doutsiopoulos. The cover art is gorgeous. It is everything I envisioned.

Thank you to my first reader, Aneta Cruz. Without a

doubt, you're my biggest cheerleader and a wonderful friend. You have taught me so much about writing. I am forever grateful.

To Deb Atwood, who I met at Better Books, thank you for reading my manuscript. I truly appreciate all your copious notes. You made my story better.

A special thank you to Tannya Derby for pointing in the right direction. Because sometimes you need to take a step back to move your story forward.

No writer is complete without their critique partners. I am fortunate to have met Catherine Arguelles, Carol Adler, Sally Spratt, and Lou Ann Barnett at the first SCBWI conference I attended. You are my writing soul sisters, and I adore each and every one of you.

A very special thank you to my dear friend, Beth McMullen. You encouraged me to think bigger and better. You are my go-to for all things publishing and for when I need a good laugh, which we both know has kept you pretty busy.

Muchas gracias to the lovely Flavia Barajas for editing the Spanish in chapter six. And thank you for helping my young reader find his way. You are an excellent teacher.

To my husband, Erik, thank you for your love and support. I could not have done this without you. You're an incredible husband and father. I appreciate all that you do every day so that I could pursue my dream. And now, at long last, I can say, "It's done."

Finally, to my son, the one and only Ollie Schmid—I wrote this for you. You inspire me every day with your silly sweetness and your kind heart. You told me to write a story, so I did. Thank you for filling my cup to the brim with happiness. I love you to the moon and back a million times.

ABOUT THE AUTHOR

Lisa Schmid is an author, a stay-at-home mom, and a pug wrangler. When she is not scaring up ghostly adventures, she is most likely scaring up fun with her husband and son. She lives in Folsom, California, home of the 1849 Gold Rush. *Ollie Oxley and the Ghost: The Search for Lost Gold* is her debut novel.